THE LOSS OF ALL LOST THINGS

AMINA

GAUTIER

ELIXIR

—

THE

LOSS

OF

ALL

LOST

THINGS

STORIES

PUBLISHED BY ELIXIR PRESS

P.O. Box 27029
Denver, Colorado 80227
www.elixirpress.com

Library of Congress Cataloging-in-Publication Data

Gautier, Amina, 1977–
[Short stories. Selections]
The loss of all lost things / Amina Gautier.
200 pages cm
ISBN 978-1-932418-56-9 (alk. paper)
I. Title.
PS3607.A976A6 2015
813'.6--dc23
2015012773

Designed by Alban Fischer
Author photo by Jenni Bryant

10 9 8 7 6 5 4 3 2 1

FIRST EDITION

CONTENTS

Introduction 1

Lost and Found 1

As I Wander 7

The Loss of All Lost Things 19

What's Best for You 31

Resident Lover 41

Directory Assistance 59

Cicero Waiting 79

A Brief Pause 91

What Matters Most 99

A Cup of My Time 117

Intersections 127

Navigator of Culture 145

Been Meaning to Say 159

Disturbance 171

Most Honest 191

INTRODUCTION

In Amina Gautier's story "Resident Lover," spurned husband Ray seeks consolation in a writing residency, where he finds himself surrounded by visual artists. He becomes infatuated with a painter named Felicia. Ray visits Felicia's studio, where he watches her work, observing that "She seemed to stand without tiring; occasionally, she perched on something, but she never fully sat down. Ray offered to fetch her stool for her, but she waved him off, saying, 'Real painters don't sit.'"

That sentiment epitomizes the stories of Amina Gautier. She does not *sit*. Just when you think that you have a bead on her vision, just when you think you know where she's coming from, she surprises and astounds you with something vaster. Whereas some writers might miniaturize, turning their own narrow life experiences into fictional texture, Gautier amplifies, using the "whole body" of literature to tell each story.

Literary fiction that grips us and won't let us go is notoriously rare. To offer us complex emotional experience *and* riveting narrative momentum, and *then* to leave the reader in contemplation of its sophisticated themes and subtle weave of objective correlatives . . . that is the stuff of literary greatness, of art that demands to be read in conversation with the canon. Yet Gautier accomplishes this feat in a way that is dynamic and fresh. There is nothing staid or old-fashioned about these stories, nothing rote or automatic.

The Loss of All Lost Things is Amina Gautier's third collection of stories. Her first book, *At-Risk*, won the Flannery O'Connor Award for Short Fiction, and her second book, *Now We Will Be Happy*, won the Prairie Schooner Book Prize. Despite these high achievements, *The Loss of All Lost Things* is in many ways Gautier's greatest book. It is certainly the most visceral and emotionally resonant.

The collection's opening story, "Lost and Found," concerns a boy who has been kidnapped by a stranger whom he calls "Thisman": "Falling into step with the boy, Thisman draws close and whispers in a voice only for him. Says, 'I wish I had a little boy just like you. I wish you were my own,' and the boy believes it, every single word." The creepiness of this opening, its unutterable mood of menace, hovers like a low cloud just above the action, threatening to rain or thunder at any moment. It never leaves you throughout the reading of the book, and even the quieter stories refuse to give comfort as we brace ourselves for the fall to come.

The Loss of All Lost Things explores loss in all of its permutations. Not just the hollowing-out loss of grief, or the flustering loss of physical things, but the loss of ideas, of potential. Nowhere is this more clear than in the story "A Cup of My Time," when Sonali learns that her gestating twins are fighting inside of her "like Jacob and Esau." She imagines "tiny little fists concealing knives, brass knuckles and nun chucks... sucker punches and black eyes and all out brawls. These twins are duking it out inside of me, kicking my ass." But the charm of the metaphor dissolves when Sonali learns from the doctor that, if the procedure fails, "You'll have to choose which one you want to live."

At the heart of these stories is the hardest of all imaginable losses: the loss of children. In the title story, a son goes missing and the parents desperately search for him, enlisting the help of friends, neighbors, and authorities, but for the parents there is no relief from the question "Where is he?" and the even more horrifying question "Whose fault is it?" "It's nothing like losing one's keys. It's not as if he has been misplaced. It's not as simple as retracing one's steps. He has not been *lost*," Gautier writes. "Lost" here would imply ownership, imply failure of responsibility, imply fault. What has happened to their son, though, is beyond words.

What Gautier achieves in *The Loss of All Lost Things* is the inverse of Ray's unfaithful wife from "Resident Lover," whose poems "could not sneak up on anyone, could not get close enough to make one flinch and could never make a person shiver. His wife's poems lacked the ability to touch the reader in any visceral way." Gautier's stories have you by the throat, and they surprise you with their mercy.

THE LOSS OF ALL LOST THINGS

LOST AND FOUND

FALLING INTO STEP with the boy, Thisman draws close and whispers in a voice only for him. Says, "I wish I had a little boy just like you. I wish you were my own," and the boy believes it, every single word.

He is lost, but not in the way he has been taught to be. Not in a supermarket; not in a shopping mall. There are no police officers or security guards to whom he can give his name and address. There is no one to page his parents over a loudspeaker to come and get him. None of the clocks where they go give the correct time and there are no calendars to mark the days. He never knows where or when he is. He remembers little of how he came to be with Thisman. He remembers only: being pulled into a car; waking up and finding himself tied to a chair in an unrecognizable room of an unfamiliar house; Thisman sitting nearby, watching and waiting; the television beside Thisman showing a movie with two naked women coiled around each another and writhing like snakes; Thisman predicting he would be a fast learner—pointing to the women, saying he would learn to do the same.

They never stay in any one place too long. They get into the car and Thisman drives. The boy is given something to drink before they leave and he never wakes until they have made it. Where they are is always secret. Sometimes it is a hotel room and they stay for weeks. Sometimes it is a borrowed house to which Thisman has the keys and they stay just long enough for the food in the fridge to spoil. In the borrowed house, Thisman feeds him soda and Cheetos for breakfast. The boy asks for cereal, milk and juice because that is what his parents give him; that is what he knows. When he mentions his parents, Thisman grows angry, cuts him off, says, "You're my little boy. I'm your father now." But Thisman looks nothing like the boy's father and—besides—his father never touches him that way.

Hardly ever is the boy left alone. He and Thisman are together everywhere they go. Unlike his parents who woke him every day only to leave him—feeding him, dressing him, rushing him only to rid themselves of him, dropping him off with strangers paid to care, and later depositing him at school in a classroom full of other left-behind boys and girls, Thisman wants him near all the time. If Thisman has a name, the boy doesn't know it. Has never been told it. Has been told not to ask. Has been told he asks too many questions. Thisman says that from now on the boy must call him Dad. If Thisman must leave, he ties the boy to a chair—twining ropes across his thighs and under the seat, across his chest and torso, and over his hands crossed at the wrists—until he returns. "Stay put," he says, as if the boy could do anything else.

Only once does Thisman forget to bind him. They are in a motel near an airfield—the boy can hear the planes as they take off and land—when Thisman decides to shower and leave the boy free. The boy waits until he hears the water running before he tries to call home. He lifts the phone's receiver and dials the only number he knows by heart. As soon as the voice says hello, the boy whispers, "I'm your son."

Someone not his parents asks, "Who is this?"

The boy says, "Come get me."

The listener hangs up. The boy does not guess that Thisman can play havoc with the phone and rearrange the numbers so that nothing matches up. Guessing the truth would only fuel the fire of his fear.

From there on out, it's easy for the boy to believe what Thisman says. And why shouldn't he? After all, his parents have never come. No one in his family wants him anymore; honestly, they never did. His parents are happy now, so much happier without him. Glad to be rid of him, they've moved on with their lives. Now they have only one child to care for, one less mouth to feed. They now spend less money on cereal and save on presents come Christmas. Now there is one less boy to whine and beg as they push the shopping cart down the aisles of the supermarket, one less child to distract them. They wouldn't want him now anyway, since he's no longer a good boy. Thisman is the only one who wants him; Thisman is the only one who loves him; Thisman is the only one who cares. The boy knows these things because Thisman tells him so, his words a litany the boy hears so often he thinks they are the thoughts inside of his own head.

Once, during his predictions, Thisman put his hand on the boy's shoulder and said, "Your little brother doesn't even remember you anymore. He thinks he's an only child. He doesn't remember a thing about having you for a brother." He'd squeezed the boy's shoulder and squinted into the distance as if he could see past the thick motel curtains and the dirty windows that were sealed shut, past the motel parking lot that he had already checked for out of town plates, past it all and straight into the boy's home—past his front door and the foyer where he always left his toys and on through the swinging door and into the kitchen and dining room where his mother sat feeding his brother. He doesn't ask how Thisman knows he has a baby brother. It confirms what he suspects. Thisman knows all; Thisman can see all things; Thisman's threats are not idle. If Thisman says that he'll kill the boy's family unless the boy behaves, the boy knows it to be so.

The television in their next motel room has just a handful of channels. The boy finds a holiday special, a not-quite cartoon with stop motion characters. A bullied reindeer has run away from home and ended up on an island of misfit toys. Each toy is defective in its own way; the choo-choo train has square wheels; the elephant is covered in polka dots; the fish flies instead of swims. Before the boy can find out what will happen to all of the rejected toys, Thisman turns the channel, flips to his favorite show.

They watch *The Twilight Zone* in every place they stay. The boy has seen enough episodes by now to have even seen some twice. Thisman has seen them all, but doesn't mind repeats. He says he's looking forward to the all-day marathon that will run in a few days—after the holidays—to bring in the New Year.

When the striped nipple cone whirls away from the star-studded screen Thisman claims to *be* Rod Serling, says that he went into hiding because the fame was too much for him to bear. This the boy does not believe. He doesn't know that Thisman isn't old enough, nor that Serling has long been dead, but he sees no resemblance between the two men. Thisman is much taller, his hair is not so severe, and he doesn't talk out of only one side of his mouth like the smirking narrator. When confronted, Thisman says it's all a ruse, says that the face he shows the boy is not his real one, says he is in disguise, says he had to change his appearance so people wouldn't recognize him. Thisman says disguises are easy to construct and that they will make one for him too. He sits in a chair and pulls the boy onto his lap. The boy squirms; he is too old for such baby treatment; he is too heavy and his legs are much longer now than when he first came, but Thisman isn't bothered. He tells him he's not heavy, he's his brother, which the boy doesn't understand at all. With one hand, Thisman squeezes the boy's thigh hard enough to bruise; with the other he smoothes the boy's hair flat. It has grown long and shaggy, which Thisman says makes him look too much like Lennon. "Time for a trim and maybe some color," Thisman announces, but they aren't going to a barbershop; Thisman will do it himself, right here and now. From his pocket come the scissors. The metal against the back of the boy's neck is cool, biting, sharp. The scissors close on a lock of the boy's hair and the hair slithers down his back and Thisman catches it and kisses it. "For a keepsake," Thisman says, holding the hair in one hand and the scissors in the other. He triggers in the boy a new fear—a fear of being slowly cut up, first his hair and then piece after piece of him until all of him has been hacked away—that makes the boy quiet and keeps him still.

When Thisman is finished, the boy looks nothing like himself, nothing like the boy in the school pictures on the desk in his father's office, the boy in the plastic sleeves within his mother's wallet, the boy beneath the strawberry-shaped magnet stuck to the refrigerator. His parents would not even recognize him now. How could they? The cuts have mostly healed but he has lost two teeth since leaving home and his hair is now a different color from when he'd first arrived; it's been cut short and dyed black, as black as Rod Serling's.

Today's episode is a new one—new for him, that is. It's all about a freckle-faced kid who controls all of the adults in his town. So far, the boy has seen episodes where the Martians trick the humans into getting on their spaceship so they can eat them, where a woman wants plastic surgery in order to have a pig nose, and where Captain Kirk sees a monster outside on the airplane wing but no one believes him, but until now he hasn't seen any episodes starring kids. The kid on the show is about his own age, yet he wields tremendous power and rules over his entire town. The boy has never ever seen a kid with that much power. The adults in the episode live in fear of the kid; they do everything to please him. They agree with him at all times. No matter what terrible thing he does, they tell him, "That was a good thing you did Anthony. A real good thing." Anytime he wants, the kid can rid himself of grown-ups by sending them to the cornfield, which the boy watching knows without being told is not a real cornfield at all but just another way of saying die—like how his teachers say passed away, like how his classmates say bought the farm and kicking up dirt. He has learned that this is something one can do with words, stretch them into softness and push them past their meaning.

Take him, for example. He prefers the word lost instead of taken. Lost is much much better. Things that are taken are never given back. Things that are lost can be found. He doesn't like to think of himself as a stolen thing, taken away in plain sight of his own home, plucked from the curb like a penny found on the sidewalk. He hates to think of himself as an easily snatched up thing—a carton of milk off a lunch tray, a pencil off a desk, a cookie from the jar. He knows that there is a place for things that are lost. He still remembers the time his father lost the car keys at the children's museum. After retracing their steps with no success, they'd gone to the Lost and Found. There, a lady pulled out a big white bin and at its bottom they found his father's keys. He remembers the Lost and Found at the school he no longer attends, the one made from the box sitting beneath his teacher's desk. Lost mittens and hats and gloves, pencil cases, notebook binders and folders all went there. It was the place to check for anything lost during class. Someone found the thing you'd lost and took it to the teacher who dropped it in the bin. When you went to look for it at the end of the day before lining up for dismissal, it was there waiting. If only he could find the Lost and Found and turn his own self in. He prefers to be lost the right way—to be deposited, placed into a bin beside all of the other lost things; he wants to sit in the plastic tub, keeping company with the keys and wallets and things that jangle that have been left behind; to take cover among the leashes and umbrellas, the glasses and the gloves, the Walkmans, sweatbands, and watches, to wait there for his parents to come and claim him—to lie safe and sound in a pile with those other missing and forgotten items, lost amongst all of the other lost things of which he is but one.

AS I WANDER

FOUR HOURS after burying Gene and Judy no longer knew what to do with herself.

She fingered the elongated leaves of her Wandering Jew plant, knowing she'd pay for it later. Touching the plants always made her itch, yet she couldn't keep away from their pointed leaves. These plants were the only things she had never killed. They grew wildly, recklessly, regardless of her tending. Despite her lack of devotion, they managed—somehow—to thrive. Sitting on a high perch above her kitchen sink, their leaves trailed over the corners of the wooden ledge. They would grow anywhere. With a bit of guidance, they'd entwine their enduring selves around anything that would let them. She took comfort in touching the hardy, invasive plant considered by all but her to be a nuisance.

Outside, it turned abruptly dark, the way it did when the season began to change. Judy could barely see the patch of yard and street beyond her window. Then, in unison, the lampposts in each home's yard flickered on, their dim lights revealing the yellow stripe in the road that divided the street in half. Old man Sampson was out there sweeping dead leaves from his stoop when a young man turned into his gate. The two spoke briefly, then went inside. Sampson left the broom by the railing and the leaves unbagged. His house was directly across the street from hers and Judy worried about his leaves blowing across and ruining her yard, which seemed more of a possibility than that the guests in her home would leave anytime soon.

She sought refuge from them in the kitchen, having been driven from all of the other rooms of her home by Gene's preying relatives. With the exception of his daughter Phoebe, Judy had never met any of them before. Gene drove them away when he first became sick, carefully and effectively cutting himself off from all of his near relatives. Now they were here, meeting her for the first time and treating her more like the hostess of a party than a bereaved wife. Some had come as mourners, others as poachers. Phoebe, who had not been over in four years, would periodically materialize at Judy's shoulder, holding a highly prized knick knack. Judy tried to avoid her, having seen the way Phoebe's eyes lingered on the china cabinet, the mirror mounted on the wall behind the sofa. She was counting, tallying up everything, quietly assessing. "When did Dad buy this?" she'd ask, suddenly appearing, fingering the costly item. She dragged her little boy all over the house, pointing out all of the possessions she assumed would soon be theirs. The four-year-old boy seemed remarkably strong and hale. Judy couldn't keep from scrutinizing him—this handsome boy that Gene had never met—wondering at Phoebe's selfishness in carrying him to term when she knew the risks, wondering how Phoebe dared.

"So this is where you disappeared to."

It was only Hank. Their neighbor and Gene's buddy, Hank had been nearby for as long as Judy could remember. Dressed in a checkered shirt, a pair of faded dungarees and work books, he looked like a man who made a living with his hands, which he was. He held a bag of ice in each hand. "What're you doing in here all by yourself?" he asked.

"Need something?"

"Everyone's looking for you," he said.

"Like who?"

"Your daughter, for one."

"Not my daughter," she said.

Hank stood quietly, adopting a silence that made her feel petty. "I'm being unfair," she said.

"That's not for me to say." He hefted the bags of ice onto the counter, dropping each one hard enough to break the ice into chunks. Hank put his hand on her waist and nudged her to the side. He reached around her, opened the silverware drawer, and pulled out a butter knife. He drove the handle of it into the belly of the ice bag. "Think about it this way," he said, pounding the ice with the base of the knife. "Tomorrow you can be anything you like."

"That's what it's all about, isn't it? Getting through this night. Fine," she said, breathing deeply. The more air she tried to take in, the tighter her chest became. "Does she have to touch everything?"

"Jude, what are you talking about?" Hank pulled a large bowl from the cupboard over the refrigerator and filled it with broken ice.

"I just can't watch her, going all over the house, touching everything. Don't you see the way her hands go all over everything?"

Phoebe was the worst of them all, but just now Judy couldn't bear to be near any of them. For hours she had listened to the memories of people she knew Gene had detested in life, yet decorum dictated she make welcome in her home. Listened as they swapped stories of a Gene she didn't know. They painted a picture of a man far different from the one she'd lived with. A man she wished she could have known. Their memories, numerous and weighty, obliterated hers.

When the bowl was filled, Hank turned back to her. "Jude. You crying?" He pulled her into an awkward hug, rubbing his cold thumbs across her upper arms.

"I'm fine. I just have to make it through tonight," she said, wiping her eyes. "But then there's tomorrow, and after that, another tomorrow. What then?"

Judy awoke to the sounds of garbage trucks approaching. She threw on a robe and ran outside. The trucks were half a block away at the corner of 43rd and Spruce. She rolled the cans to the curb, noticing all of the cans lining the fronts of all of the other homes. It was eight AM and she had not seen any cans on the curb the night before. When, she wondered, had everyone else come out with their trash?

If she had let him, Hank would have put out the garbage for her. When she returned home at daybreak, she'd heard his voice message offering to do just that. Because Gene could no longer do it, Hank had taken over performing the small odd jobs necessary for maintaining a home. For the past four years, he'd sprayed weed killer on the lawn during the spring and summer. In the winter he'd bled the radiators and shoveled the snow. Each year, Judy watched him take what looked like an old roller skating key and move among all of their old radiators, letting out air and steam. While each radiator hissed and sputtered, Judy would look at Hank, resplendent in health and heartiness and wonder why Gene had not been spared instead. She resented his min-istrations—the way he hefted bags of ice and pounded them to shards against the counter, the familiarity he had with his own body, the way he could walk without jerking, the ease of his well meaning smile—simple things over which Gene had long ago lost mastery.

She'd been out when Hank called about the garbage. In the month since Gene's death, Judy had taken to wandering the neighborhood whenever the mood took her. Though she'd lived in the University City/West Philadelphia area since her marriage, she'd never really seen it. She'd given up her apartment in Rittenhouse Square when she'd married Gene and she had never spent much time in West Phil-adelphia prior to dating him. Gene began a progressive decline shortly after their marriage five years ago and most of her time had been spent visiting him in the hospital or providing full-time care for him inside their home. The neighborhood was not a place she associated with him. They'd taken no strolls past the University of Pennsylvania and visited none of the restaurants that surrounded it on Sansom, Walnut and Chestnut. They had watched no movies at the Cinemagic or the new theater, The Bridge. None of these places reminded her of Gene. Unlike home, they held no memories for her, so she frequented them. Wandering kept her away from home, freeing her from condolence cards, visits, and phone calls, the wounding sympathy of others.

After hearing Phoebe's voice message asking if she could come by, Judy had left the house and gone to Clark Park. She had no desire to see Gene's daughter. She went to the park in only a black fleece; she'd taken no jacket. She'd ordered the fleece for him from an online catalogue. Gene liked the way it fit across his shoulders and took to wearing it constantly. Even when it was stained and dirty, he took no notice of the offending dirt or odor and wore it blithely. Eventually, it became too baggy for him and hung from his thinning frame and still he wore it.

She'd sat on a bench in the park until the sun came up. During the day, people brought their dogs to the park and on the weekends, it became one giant flea market, but late at night it was a place for transients. Judy sat there until the last owners took their dogs home, until the last grad students headed back to their apartments, until the last families bundled up their children and took them away, until the last couples stopped kissing, and waited. She watched them all leave, some getting into their cars, some boarding the trolleys on Baltimore and Chester Avenues, and some simply walking. Then she made her way deeper into the large park. West Philadelphia's homeless buried themselves in the park's recesses, away from the vigilance of campus security bike patrollers who swarmed the park's perimeters, bent on protecting students who lived off campus. Judy selected a bench among them and huddled. She had lost her ability to find anything disgusting in mingling among those whom she would have normally avoided. Most, she guessed, were addicts or mentally ill, but she made no distinction between herself and them. Life had stolen something from them, robbed them, made them crazy and despairing so that they cared only for something to distract them. The park had become a depository for the unwanted, forgotten, and discarded. Sitting there in Gene's extra large fleece, Judy pulled her arms deep within the sleeves and laid herself down among them, wrapped in the fleece full of Gene's funk.

Gene had said he would not leave her before it was his time to go and she had believed him.

The next morning, when she made it the few blocks back home, there had been no garbage cans on the curbs, yet now here they were. Across the street, Old man Sampson bumped a shopping cart down his front steps. Haphazardly thrown into the cart were hardback books without covers, institutional copies. She assumed he was going to campus to return them. Why he did not pack them into bags, she did not know. The books, jumbled as they were, poked through the spaces in his cart. With every bump of the wheel against the concrete steps, the pile jostled and tomes threatened to slip out.

No garbage cans lined Sampson's curb. After he pushed his cart down the street and crossed it, Judy thought how neighborly it would have been of her to remind him of garbage day.

Later that day, Judy brought out a folding chair and placed it on her top step. From her vantage point, she'd be able to see Sampson's return. She would apologize for not reminding him about the garbage and assume responsibility for him suffering the inconvenience of keeping his trash around an extra week. Judy knew little of him, only that he was a retired professor, that he lived alone, and that he had an abundance of young male visitors. Gene had not liked him. Since she'd taken to wandering, she'd seen the parade of young black boys going in and out of the old man's house at all hours of the night. To Judy, they seemed impossibly young and thuggish, arrogantly rough. Small and wiry, they were none of them over six feet tall. Judy was no fool. She knew Sampson's preferences, but it was not her place to judge.

The 42 bus was at the top of the hill inching its way down Spruce when a young man jogged up Sampson's steps, rang the bell and waited.

"He's not home!" Judy yelled.

The boy looked for the voice. She stood and waved until he noticed her.

He crossed the street. "You say something to me?"

"Sampson's not home."

"He always home."

"I saw him leave earlier," she said. "He had a cart full of books."

"Oh," the boy said, as if that explained everything. He was standing at the edge of her steps.

"Are you his nephew?"

"Nah," he said. "I ain't related to that boy." In his mouth boy sounded like ball.

"Do you work for him, then?" she asked.

He wore a du-rag on his head and was dressed in a long plain white tee shirt that came down to his knees, and a pair of baggy jeans barely visible beneath the tee shirt, looking like so many other young boys she had seen all over West Philadelphia, indistinct and indistinguishable. His youth clung to him, a mixture of freshness, arrogance and bravado. He smirked. "Work for him? Yeah. You could say that."

Judy had seen the old man a scant number of times and had spoken to him but once. His voice had been gravelly, reminding her of Louis Armstrong's. On the rare occasions she did see him, he made her think of a turtle with his shy and slow ways, his heavy lidded eyes and wide wide mouth. She could not picture him and this insolent youth together.

"He forgot to take out his trash today," she said.

The youth shrugged. "I don't do garbage. How long ago you say he left?"

"About two hours, I guess."

"Shit."

"I guess he'll be back soon," Judy said.

The boy looked at his watch. "He ain't coming back for hours." He turned to go. Judy didn't want him to. He was the first person, other than Hank, that she'd spoken with in all of the days that made up the month that it had been since Gene's passing.

"You ever read any Baldwin?" she asked.

"Nah. Who's that?"

"I would imagine that Sampson has a lot of interesting books."

"I don't read when I'm over there." He smirked again and hitched his pants, giving Judy what she supposed was meant to be a belligerently knowing stare. She saw only the awkward patch of dark hairs above the bridge of his nose where his brows connected. The boy held a toothpick between teeth that were strong and white. She guessed he'd wanted to make her uncomfortable, but she felt only a rush of desire for the arrogant and impervious youth.

"You can wait in here for him if you'd like."

He followed her in and moved through her house as if he'd been in it a hundred times, making a circuit through her enclosed porch, living room and dining room, picking up things and looking at them as he went.

"Does Sampson's house look like this?" she asked.

"Kind of, but he's got more junk and shit than you," he said. "He never clean up. There be like papers everywhere. I gotta step all over them. I try to be careful, but sometimes it's like too many and I step on one and then he get all crazy—be like 'That's my conference paper from 1992!' and I be like damn nigga if it's that important why you got it lying all on the floor and shit? Pick that shit up, then!" He stopped abruptly, as if realizing he'd said too much. He patted the couch and sat down. "Nah, this here is real clean," he said. "Real nice." He picked up the universal remote control and turned on the TV without asking. He skipped through the channels before finally settling on some sort of reality show. From what Judy could tell, the premise of the show was for young and uncouth women to attend a version of charm school in order to compete for the hand of a former rapper who lacked charm himself.

"So, where your husband at?" he asked.

"I buried him last month."

"My bad," he said, not looking away from the TV screen. "You ain't got no pictures of him up nowhere."

The sicker Gene had become, the more he'd refused to take pictures with her since he could not be sure to smile. His face seemed to settle into a permanent grimace he could neither feel nor control. "Remember me the way I was when I met you," he would say whenever Judy tried to change his mind. She had only two pictures with Gene, their wedding photo and a picture that had been taken of them on the Spirit of Philadelphia. She'd removed those pictures from the living room before the wake and had put them upstairs in her bedroom. In both pictures, Gene had been smiling.

"I don't like taking pictures," Judy said.

The youth shrugged and put his feet on the coffee table.

Judy waited for him to ask what Gene had died of and thought of how to answer, but the boy switched to another reality show about students at a historically black college and became engrossed.

She asked how much Sampson paid him, and it was very little. She removed the money from her wallet and laid it on the table by his feet. He looked at her until she began to feel she had erred. Then he crushed the bills in his hands and shoved them deep into his pocket.

She gestured for him to remove the black nylon stocking cap tied around his head. Beneath the du-rag, his long hair was braided in a complex pattern with two whorls on either side that reminded her of ram's horns. Judy lightly touched his hair, finding it as soft and downy as a child's.

He pulled her hand away. "Don't touch me," he said. "And no marks either."

"Okay," Judy said. She thought of stipulating her own conditions for protection, then decided she had nothing to lose.

After taking off his du-rag, he removed the rest of his clothing, revealing a lanky frame. His legs were long, his calves small hard knobs protruding from the backs of bony legs. She pulled his face to her and kissed him hard and tasting. His lips were soft and fleshy, unlike the rest of him. He was surprisingly gentle and silent within her. She'd expected the inadequacy of youth, the exaggerated violence of the disadvantaged. She'd wanted to be an outlet for his unleashed anger, had prepared for it, hoped it would cleanse her of her own.

If she was angry, she had no one to blame for it but herself.

Though she'd married late in life, their marriage had been her first. It had been Gene's second. By the time they'd met, Judy had convinced herself she was bored with the formalities of dating and she cared more for companionship than courting. She and Gene had dated a mere three months. She had not been deceived. She had known what she was getting into. She knew Gene was getting sick, knew she loved him, knew he hadn't wanted to die alone. Three months or three years of dating would not have changed her feelings or her decision. Some called it selfish and calculating. His family accused her of lying in wait, marrying him just because he was dying. Once he'd gotten sick, they'd wanted to lock him away in a nursing home and wait for him to die. They behaved as if he were a nuisance. Judy was his protection, his shield against a lonely death.

She had not thought of needing her own protection. Of course she had known that Gene would die before her, but she had not known how it would feel once the empty days came. She'd thought that she could prepare for it, keep it from touching her as deeply as she'd suspected it was able.

The boy's eyes, liquid black, were focused on something just over her shoulder. His body seemed to move of its own accord. He seemed oddly untouched, detached from the manipulations of his body, as if sex were something one did rather than something one had. Somewhere, in his own neighborhood, he had a girlfriend whom he did not think of at times like this. Somewhere, he had a separate life that he kept intact. Like her, he foolishly believed he had an impenetrable core that defined him, shielded him from his outward self, kept him from being touched.

In minutes he was asleep, his legs carelessly anchoring her. Judy touched his face, finding it remarkably smooth. She'd loved all the lines on Gene's face. Summers spent down on the beaches of the Jersey shore had not been kind to Gene, but she'd loved the deep creases of the premature wrinkling that had given his face character.

It was unfair, Gene had said, meeting her at a time like that. He'd said he wished he had the proper time to court her, said they shouldn't lose a single day together. The man that had finally taken his own life rather than continue to waste away was not her husband. Gene had promised not to so long as Judy didn't put him away. She'd kept her word, relying upon the tenuous love of the dying man who had taken all of their remaining days, all of their tomorrows, and left her with only promises, fragile as strands of hair.

The boy jerked under her hand, and Judy touched his hair lightly, soothingly, her fingers wandering over his intricately patterned corn-rows, following their winding paths along the contour of his head to the base of his skull where they curled under at the ends. Once he quieted, Judy grasped the soft and tenuous braids, undoing the plait-ed strands.

THE LOSS OF ALL LOST THINGS

THE POSTERS go up immediately.

They search in all weather; they harass the media for coverage. They leave the light on outside. They do not touch their answering machine: they keep the message exactly the same. They supply the authorities with recent photos, with medical and dental records, with everything they ask. They do all they can think of. They never rest. They never tire. They never lose hope.

They take time off, calling in vacation and sick days so that they can stay home and wait, so they can go out and search, so that they can focus on what's most important. So understanding, their friends and neighbors. The whole neighborhood turns out again and again to help them search. There are flyers, cadaver dogs, groups pairing off with flashlights. T-shirts and buttons, posters and ribbons. They turn their house over to the recovery enterprise, transforming their den, basement and garage into a headquarters to take the calls that stream in and handle the volunteers who show up. Her sister and brother-in-law are a godsend for the two weeks they're in town. They drive in from out of state, ready to help. Her sister keeps an eye on their younger son, supplies coffee and donuts to the volunteers. Her brother-in-law mans the phones, listens to the callers and handles the cranks.

It's not as if he has been misplaced. It's nothing like losing one's keys. It's not as simple as retracing one's steps. He has not been *lost*, but the proper word is too dirty a word that makes it all too real, makes them dread instead of hope. Whose fault is it? He was on no one's watch. Less than a block between the school bus drop-off point and home, grabbed somewhere in between.

They put up more posters each time they leave the house. How she hates to see them preyed upon by the elements: blowing down the street, crumpled at the curb, blasted by the rain, faded by the sun. Stapled to lampposts and trees, the posters are no match for the passage of time. The sight of one dumped into the public garbage can on their street—her son's face peering through the metal latticework—is enough to send her back indoors, where she will lock herself in and not venture out for days.

It's no better inside. She cannot look anywhere without seeing him. His face is in her wallet, preserved behind a plastic sheath. She sees his picture on the refrigerator, peeking out beneath a strawberry-shaped magnet. Scattered through the foyer are all of his toys—she sees them every time she hangs her coat. She refuses to let their younger son play with them. She tells herself they have too many moving pieces, too many small parts a young child could swallow, but—truly—she just cannot stand to see a single toy moved from its spot. Only by leaving each one exactly where her older son left it can she maneuver through her day, logging into her computer and searching for news, printing the never-ending flyers, closing her eyes to all of the false leads that cruelly continue to come in.

They count his absence in days, the way parents count the age of infants in months, hoping the incremental tallying will somehow make time slow down, make the seconds add up less quickly. They use the holidays as milestones. Halloween and Thanksgiving come and go. Surely, they predict, he'll be home by Christmas. They decorate, slip presents under the tree. When Christmas comes and goes, they hold out for New Year's Day.

Thirty days. Seventy-five. One hundred twenty days and still count-ing. One hundred eighty three days. Saying it that way makes it seem like so much less than half a year.

Whose fault is it? Who would do such a thing? They blame television. They blame drugs and pornography for warping the minds of many. They blame sexual deviance and mental illness. Greed. Selfishness. Loneliness. Perversion. There are any number of reasons; the guess-ing only makes it worse. Too late do they learn to be wary. They peer into the eyes of every person they meet; anyone between the ages of eighteen and eighty is fair game. The two men who haul their garbage. The guy who delivers their pizza. It doesn't even have to be a strang-er. Everyone is suspect. The young man who shovels their neighbor's snow, the youth pastor who dresses better than he should, the teacher's aide who once gave their son a ride home.

"It could be a woman," she interjects. She latches onto the idea, conjures the tale of a desperate woman who looks at their boy and sees the child she lost long ago. Their boy is just the age her miscarried child would have been had it lived. In a crazed moment, she steals him. She calls him by her own son's name, forces him to answer. Soon she doesn't remember that he's not really hers.

"Don't talk like that," her husband says.

"I can't help it," she says. Truly, she can't. She can't stop talking like this, can't stop thinking like this. By now she knows the statistics, knows the likely profile. Her brain is filled with information she nev-er wanted. Eighty percent of abductors have normal IQs or higher. There are over 600,000 registered sex offenders in the United States. Most abductors are not "dirty old men" as popularly believed—sev-enty percent are younger than thirty-five years of age, seventy percent are younger than her. She soothes herself with the safest of fantasies, hoping for the least of all the evils. By now she knows how slim the chance is, but she prefers to think of this desperate woman, who would treat their son like her own. Is she feeding him properly? Is he warm enough at night?

"He'll be wearing new clothes when we get him back. Some weird tacky getup she's dressed him in, some dowdy thing she thinks matches." Their older boy's clothes wait in the hamper. They won't wash them until he's back. He has missed three haircuts and one dental appointment. She wonders aloud if the desperate woman will see to it.

He rises from the table, his hands covering his ears. He doesn't sing or hum to tune her out, but he might as well. In no time he is halfway down the hall and into the bedroom that they no longer share. She hears the door slam shut.

"That's right, leave," she says. "Run!"

She searches the kitchen cabinet, looking for a little liquid courage. Where is all the damn liquor?

Her younger son enters the kitchen carrying a green ogre action figure in one hand and a gray plastic donkey in the other.

"Where'd you get those?"

"On the floor."

"You put those right back where you found them."

He shakes his head. "I wanna play with them."

"They're your brother's." She snatches the toys from his hands and runs out to the foyer, where she scans the floor and tries to remember where they were meant to go. "Where were they? How were they? Show me!"

Her younger son bursts into tears.

"Get in here and show me!" she demands.

Her younger son points to an area near the front window and another near the doorway. "Which one?" she asks, holding both toys aloft.

He points to the spot by the front entrance and mumbles, "The Greenie goes there."

She lays the green ogre down near the umbrella stand. "Like this?" She kneels on the carpet and positions him on his back, remembering that she had seen him that way, his hands stretched up toward the ceiling. She looks at him lying like that and knows something is wrong. The ogre's right hand should be positioned slightly lower than its left. She adjusts the toy until she's satisfied. Guided by her son, she crawls to the spot by the window, maneuvering around the other strewn toys—a video game controller, a soft foam football, a tiny-headed dinosaur— and places the donkey on its side as she had last remembered seeing it. Only when both toys are in their proper places does she stand up and walk away.

Her younger son cries anew. "But I wanna play with them!"

"Wait until your brother gets back," she says, as if his older brother is just down the street at a friend's house, as if he will be back any minute now, or at least in time for dinner, as if the streetlights coming on at all of the nearby curbs will be the signal for him that it is for all of the other children, urging them inside for the night.

Her younger son retreats to the kitchen and kicks the chairs. His tears become shrieks as he demands to know where his big brother is, and why he can't play with the toys. The urge to soothe him is strong, but she resists. In his eyes, she sees her lost boy looking back. She calls for her husband, asks him to calm the boy. But it is too late. Their younger son hurts himself with crying, strangles himself on saliva, coughs and chokes on his tears. Over his head, they look at one another and make their decision. How are they to focus on recovering their lost boy if they have to worry about this one too? They cannot love him right now. Wisely, they refrain. It's not fair with the older one missing. So they pack him up, tell him he is going to visit with his aunt and uncle. They let him take as many of his own toys as he would like. They promise to see him soon, but they never tell him when.

They are not the first to suffer loss. They try to keep it all in perspective, to think of the myriad things that have been lost. *Such as:*

The Ark of the Covenant. The city of Atlantis. The Dead Sea

Scrolls. El Dorado. The Holy Grail. Amelia Earhart, somewhere over the Pacific. Pompeii, buried beneath volcanic ash. The RMS Titanic, at the bottom of the sea.

Other lost things are lost slowly, over time, rather than in one fell swoop. *Such as:*

Loss of feeling, of life and limb. Loss of blood. Loss of memory. Loss of looks, of faith and time. Loss of sanity. Teeth lost under the pillow. Long-lost relatives—ignored, forgotten, and pretended away.

They make these lists to humble themselves, remembering the way their parents attempted to cure picky eating habits with reminders of children starving in Africa, but the shaming tactic doesn't work. Try as they might to think of others who have it worse, all that they can think of is themselves.

The missing, the absence, the waiting, takes their toll. In the beginning, they spent all of their time searching, but the exhaustion of daily life has overtaken them. They cannot do nothing but search. They must eat, they must sleep. Certainly they do not indulge—no parties, no movies, no dancing—but once in a while they do turn on the television. They opt for marathons—*I Love Lucy, The Twilight Zone, The Honeymooners,* and sit through them unblinking. If ever they forget, lose themselves in the moment and laugh at something on the screen, they use these momentary lapses as ammunition, firing against each other. *How can you laugh at a time like this? How can you eat? How can you sleep?* They hate each other for their weakness, for the living that muscles through.

Blame is the glue that keeps them together. They shuttle it between them, neither one able to shoulder it alone. Their first child was born to bind them, to transform them from *couple* into *family,* yet his absence is what renders them inseparable. They cannot endure this without each other. Splitting up is too simple of a solution. Far too easy to buckle beneath the strain of it all. If one of them should leave before their boy returns? Neither wants to miss the homecoming. So she moves into their older son's bedroom and he stays put. He will not go and she will not make him. They cannot afford it. Their paid time off has run out; they've used up all of their leave; they're depleting their savings; soon they will be eating away at the money set aside for their retirement. They are in too deep for either of them to take a step alone. They are stuck. Stuck here. Stuck in this time. Stuck together. Whose fault is it? It's been so long now they no longer know.

Worse than mourning is this waiting that never ends.

No longer so understanding, their supporters. The encouraging letters from people they have never met stop coming in batches; only a handful trickle in. The media has moved on, covering newer stories. Their neighbors, who have long since returned to their own lives, pester them to say the words. Their friends, relatives, and loved ones who wanted them to remain hopeful now want them to admit that the worst has come. There is no more pretending. Three hundred days now. So much time has passed, too much to expect anything good. There are people who can help them, their supporters say—professionals to whom they can turn. Therapists, pastors, prayer circles, and grief counselors. But they'd prefer to keep their grief to themselves. They don't want to share their misery, hand it off to others, or have it counseled away. It's all they have left of him. They keep it to themselves, feeding and sucking on who they are—the parents of a lost boy. Their status gives them a Get Out of Jail Free card to be miserable, to be any way they want. Their misery is nourishing; they fill up on it. Rather than put it away, they prefer to live in limbo, in this new waiting world where they have not wronged each other, in this world where no one cares about all of the ways they have erred. In this limbo life, the only thing that matters is their boy. They do not have to be good people; they are not held accountable for what they say and do. As the parents of the lost boy they are entitled to a break.

Deep in the deepest deepness of their hearts, there lies a relief to which they will never own up, this consolation that just right now they do not have to look at themselves too closely. They'd never been perfect parents to begin with, but there is no time now for past hurt, no room for grudges, no space to allow old resentments or unfinished business. To nurse wounds from their private lives at a time like this is pettiness plain and simple. Their boy is all that matters. Those times when he turned to other women, many other women, many other times; the one time she'd turned to one other man, deliberately to balance the scale—all those times when they chose to hurt each other with indifference, negligence, and silence, are now packed away with the summer clothes they have finally washed, the ones their older son will have outgrown by the time they get him back. Those wounds are tucked into the trunk with the clothes they will save for their remaining son to grow into; those hurts are wedged in tightly among the mothballs. They will deal with those later, unpack the hurts and air everything out. For now, they will simply stay.

He loses sleep. Earlier that afternoon she saw a discarded poster; now her crying keeps him awake all night, drywall and plaster no match for her tears. He gets up from the bed they no longer share and crosses to his older son's room to check on her. He hasn't minded the new sleeping arrangements. Secretly, he blames her a little more than himself for what has happened, but he isn't thinking this when he touches her wet face. They'd agreed to abstain, unable to bear the idea of sex at a time like this, feeling like perverts every time they sought to console themselves with their bodies, took pleasure in rubbing against one another, in delving into one another while their boy was out there missing. Tonight, he decides, is an exception. He lifts her—she is so light now—and carries her to their bedroom, settling her into a bed from which she has too long been absent.

Into the dark, against the curve of his neck, she whispers, "Find me." Urges him on, saying, "I want you to lose me and then find me." She is trying to say what she cannot say, but lost in the moment of rekindled pleasure, all he hears is what sounds like her talking crazy. They have sad sorrowful sex, making a love that leaves them feeling worse. When they are through, their thoughts remain troubled as ever. They hate and they love. They do not know why, but they feel it and they are in agony.

Immediately after, she peels him off her like a top sheet and slips from his embrace, making it back to the other room without having to be carried. She tucks herself back into the other bed, the one too small and narrow for her body. The other night, she'd fallen asleep in the den, in front of the TV, while watching a special on lost cities. She'd tuned in just as a row of plaster casts in the shape of human bodies was being shown. The narrator said that the victims were *in situ*, still lying in the positions they'd been in when they'd died. She'd powered off the television after that, unable to watch any more. Now she imagines that their home is one of those homes in that Roman city that the archaeologists found lost under layers of civilizations and her body is one of the bodies they discovered buried beneath the ash. Her older son's return will be her excavation. That is when she will be unearthed and brought once more to the surface and to the light. Right now she is buried beneath the tephra; she is an artifact for study. Who will inject the plaster, the resin, so that she can take shape and discover who she used to be?

In this room, she is free to count her losses. She was ten years old when she lost a birthday card with a ten dollar bill taped inside. Fifteen when she lost her first ever camera. Nineteen when she lost her virginity and she still wants it back. But no other loss compares to the loss of one small boy, and losing him makes her feel all of the other losses once more. Each loss is a reprimand, a reminder of her helplessness; each loss is a disorienting thing. Each loss, its own little death. She feels each loss so keenly, huddling there beneath her older son's blanket, crushed and cowered by the loss of all lost things.

He knocks, pushes open the unlocked door. He comes carrying her planner and sees the covered mound on the bed that is her body hidden and shrouded beneath their son's thin blanket. He turns on the lamp by the bed, pulling on the tiny starfish at the end of the chain. He smoothes his hands over her silhouette, touching the prone and still body, trying to find where she begins. He searches her out beneath the covers, finds the edge of the blanket and slowly tugs. Bit by bit he reveals her—bringing head, shoulder, arms, torso, and all the rest to light, until no part of her is left lost beneath, until she has been unearthed.

He has found her, just as she'd asked.

She blinks at the brightness of the room. "Maybe we made a mistake to—"

Against her lips, he presses a finger that seems to say *Perhaps we made a mistake, but by now there have been too many mistakes for us to count.*

She makes room and he climbs into the twin-sized bed beside her, squeezing in and pressing his back against the wall until they both fit. Together, they make a plan for the future. They want to be happy again. They do not know when they will finally get their lost son back, but they will all need a fresh start whenever he returns. In the meantime, their younger son must come home. They agree to collect him first thing in the morning. They don't want to lose him to another day.

Refusing to look at all of the squares filled with X's marking the days their older son has been gone, they flip past the months-at-a-glance portion of the calendar and instead go straight to the back of the book, to the supplemental pages for names and numbers. The year-at-a-glance calendars for the current and next two years are condensed on the lefthand side and on the opposite page, a map of the United States is bracketed and coded to delineate the different time zones and area codes.

Let them start anew.

Poring over the planner, they consider the geometry of states, and wonder where they might go. They will pick a state—any state—and once they are all together they will head out for it and hold it to its promise. There, in that new place, they will all be new people. Where shall it be? They close their eyes. He places his hand atop hers and they move their index fingers across the map. Blindly, they point. When they open their eyes, they sound out the name beneath their fingers, trying its newness on for size.

WHAT'S BEST FOR YOU

HERE IS BERNICE in mid-afternoon, filling a two-shelved cart with books checked out through Inter Library Loan. Down they will go to Circulation, where they will be left for patrons who live too near to have their books mailed. It's really a job for the work-study students, but they're in the mailroom at this time of day, packaging fifty pound boxes bound for the other Ivies. Once they get the shipment ready for UPS, they'll return. Bernice doesn't mind doing this herself. She could use the exercise.

(There are some unkind souls who would call Bernice fat, but it's all a matter of how you look at things.)

But first, her daily call to check on Melanie. After four rings, Bernice hears her own voice telling her to leave a message.

You've reached Melanie and Bernice. Unfortunately,
we are unable to take your call. Please leave us a
message after the tone. Thank you and God bless.

How dull her own voice sounds. A few weeks ago, Melanie changed the message without her knowledge and until Bernice caught it, callers had received the cryptic message: *Do what you do.*

Which is precisely what Bernice is afraid of, that her fifteen-year-old daughter is out somewhere, *doing.*

She still remembers the time when an eight-year-old Melanie began to play with the new boy across the hall. Bernice had thought to give her "The Talk," but no sooner had she had the thought than her mind protested *Too soon! Too soon!* One talk like that would lead to another and another and all of the talks would lead to Melanie growing up too fast. So she had kept silent and the boy's mother later caught them playing doctor. She still remembers the fifth grade teacher who took Melanie to the bathroom when she first menstruated. Bernice had been ready that time, but still too late. She'd bought a book featuring black and white naked photos of unsmiling teenagers taken during the different stages of puberty. She'd been impressed by the austere expressions on the faces of the generic white models, thinking they would convey to Melanie the idea that puberty was serious business. Bernice presented Melanie with the book and a package of sanitary napkins, only to watch her daughter flip through the photos with disinterest, world weary at the age of eleven.

Where Melanie goes and what she does during the hours between the time school lets out and Bernice gets home is a mystery. Melanie has no after school activities. She plays no sports and her best friend Chandra has to stay twice a week to keep out of summer school. So there is nothing to keep her.

Bernice hangs up and her thoughts turn to dinner. She is thinking of steak smothered in onions and peppers. Of crisp green beans. Of mashed potatoes and gravy. She is thinking of cling peaches in their own syrup poured over pound cake. She always cooks for two, though Melanie only nibbles. If it were left up to her daughter, they would never eat anything that took longer than five minutes to prepare. Melanie could live happily off of only macaroni and cheese, but Bernice believes in full meals, not the side dishes Melanie prefers. If it were left up to Melanie, Bernice would not be allowed to eat anything at all.

Bernice wheels her cart around the long way, moving surreptitiously through the stacks until she sees Harold's mop at the PS.153's. The third floor of the library is nearly vacant at this time of the day. Harold sneaks breaks into his cleaning circuit, stopping to read whatever catches his interest. He likes long books, Bernice knows, books he can't possibly finish during his shift. She has seen him photocopying chapters. She has seen him with tubes of rolled papers in his back pocket, mopping without a care. She has seen him—watched him actually—enough times to place him in his late forties, to find him handsome and well-preserved despite the beginnings of a bald spot, to wish that she could swallow his songs.

It seemed to Bernice that Harold was simply there one day instead of Elsie, the usual cleaning person.

She was leaning over the sink brushing her teeth after lunch when he knocked on the door and entered the women's restroom before she could answer.

"What are you doing in here?"

He gestured to the mop and the bucket on wheels. "Cleaning."

"What happened to Elsie?"

"You mean the retarded girl?"

"I don't like to use that word," Bernice said. When Bernice first met her, she'd mistaken her slow and simple deliberate speech for that of a non-native speaker, but soon realized her error. Bernice was used to Elsie in her baggy gray sweat suits, moving through the library with her mop and its bucket on wheels. She talked to any and every one who'd tolerate her. The students mostly ignored her, but Bernice was always kind.

Harold held his hand high over his head, jostling the spray bottle of disinfectant hooked onto his belt loop by its nozzle. "The real big girl?"

"She is very tall," Bernice conceded, guessing Harold to be around 5′9″. Elsie was a good six feet.

"She bit someone," he said. "Right on the cheek."

"I don't believe you," she said. She lifted her hand to her own cheek, staggered by the intimacy of the violent act, knowing how close you had to get to a person to bite someone on the face. She herself had not been that close to anyone in some time. "So they suspended her? When will she be back?"

"She's not coming back. Not back here anyway," he said. "No sir. She's gone for good."

"But why? All of the workers here know that she's... not quite right. Maybe it wasn't her fault. Medicine or something," Bernice said, knowing there was no medicine for what was wrong with Elsie. "Maybe it was a mistake."

Harold shrugged. "Maybe. But she didn't bite a worker. She bit a student."

It wasn't fair, Bernice thought. People could do anything they wanted to a tenured professor who had been teaching at the university for over twenty years and no one would blink an eye. They could hold a staff member hostage and walk away Scot free. But let someone so much as sneeze on one of the four year students who entered and left the university through revolving doors and all hell broke loose. Recyclable, replaceable and reusable as they were, these disposable students were handled as if precious and fine, their well-being much more important than that of the permanent members of the university community.

No one ever saw Elsie again. Now there is only Harold. Harold with his sweet songs.

This time, it is Donny Hathaway. Bernice recognizes "A Song for You."

In the corridor off of the restrooms, there is only the sound of Harold's voice and the hum of the photocopier. No one else hears his sweet tenor but Bernice.

Harold opens the hardbound book, parting its pages at the middle, holding the book with two hands before turning it over and pressing it upon its face against the glass of the photocopier, its spine high in the air. He licks his finger and runs it down the groove of the spine, applying gentle pressure. He never closes the lid on the book. Instead, he places his palm lightly on the book's back, holding it in place, gently aligning.

As Harold sings about acting out his love in stages, his hands—gentle with the books—are telling Bernice, telling her, telling her just how it could be.

"Harold?"

He turns, looking sheepish. "Don't quit my day job, right?"

She has not meant to say his name or speak at all. Now she feels she should say something, ask him a question, tell him there is a spill that needs attention. "No," she says. "It's lovely."

He smiles, revealing capped white teeth. "Thanks." Bernice doesn't notice the smile, or the way it takes years off his face. Her eyes are riveted to his hand, which remains on the book, fingers idly caressing.

Bernice wheels her cart to the elevator, pressing DOWN. A month ago, soon after he'd first arrived, Harold had hit on her. She'd run into him at these same elevators, only that time she'd been on her way up to Special Collections.

"Your hair is different today," he'd said. "It looks nice."

Bernice had raised a hand to her hair, then dropped it when she realized what she'd done. "Thank you."

"Do you ever go to the Food Court? It's nearby. I thought we could get some lunch."

"Well, I usually bring in my own meals," Bernice said. "I'm on a diet."

"A diet?"

"Yes."

Harold's eyes slid down her body, giving her the once over. "Only a dog wants a bone."

Jacob is at Circulation today. He holds the swinging door open for Bernice and she wheels her cart behind his desk to the little room at the back, hardly noticing him.

Unlike Reference, Circulation and Information, all mixed groups, there are only women in Inter Library Loan. Bernice doesn't know why this is, only that it is so. They are all white, except for her. Until Harold came, Bernice was the only black person on the entire third floor. Though she has not previously given it much thought, it takes Harold's being there to make her see that she has been virtually alone.

She'd missed her chance with Harold that day, but she doesn't imagine she won't get another one. She can do something about it. Take him up on the offer. Today. Why not today?

Bernice nestles her cart in a corner. Exchanging it for an empty one, she goes back out the way she came.

It doesn't have to be lunch. It could be dinner. *She* doesn't have to go straight home, Bernice reminds herself. She doesn't have a curfew.

Back in her own office, she calls her daughter, feeling like a teenager asking for permission to stay out later. There has never been a day Melanie has come home to an empty house or a cold stove, not that she appreciates it. She usually slings her books onto the nearest chair, eats as quickly as possible and then runs back outside where the boys she dates are waiting with their cars. Once, watching from the window, Bernice saw Melanie waiting at the curb. A black Oldsmobile slowed down and honked. Melanie waved to the driver, jumped in and sped away. The next day, over breakfast, Melanie laughed at her when she suggested that the next time a boy picked her up, Melanie wait for her date to get out and open her door.

"That's so over. We're not in the fifties," Melanie said, dumping her cereal bowl into the sink. "Things have changed."

"Some things never do," Bernice said, running water in the bowl and washing it clean with a soap-filled sponge. "Men today want what they wanted back then. And I did not grow up in the fifties. You know that."

"Fifties, sixties, whatever. That was then. Besides, Bernice, what would you know about it?" Melanie said, never ever calling her Mom. "It's not like I'm doing anything anyway."

She was lying. Bernice could tell by the way Melanie walked now, conscious of her hips, rolling them with every step as if she were made of pulleys. Melanie met her eyes now without fear. No longer full of innocence, her brown eyes reflected a daunting and new awareness that made the hairs rise at the back of Bernice's neck.

Bernice blames herself.

It is her fault for being too simple. For having been raised on notions and whispered half-truths. She had been brought up on the silence of adults and on the unsolicited advice of worldly cousins. For the longest time, she had believed that urinating or douching immediately after sex would prevent pregnancy. She had listened to all the whispers, believing that the white splotches on her fingernails represented the number of boyfriends she would have, believing that hiccups indicated she was growing taller, believing that if she stepped on a crack it would break her mother's back.

No one answers the phone.

You've reached Melanie and Bernice. Unfortunately,
we are unable to take your call. Please leave us a
message after the tone. Thank you and God bless.

When did she become that voice on the machine? When had she begun to sound just like a librarian? She wanted to believe that the dullness had crept up on her, slowly eroding her personality at the edges until she was the new blunted and smoothed over version of herself, when she knew that the truth was she had always been this way. Even as a child. She had never been a quick study like Melanie. Never been rebellious. Never tested the limits. Whenever she had misbehaved, someone had always been there to discipline her. They used to make her pick out her own switch from the yard. Dutifully, she'd pick a young yet firm one and let herself be whipped with the switch of her choice rapping across her buttocks and stinging the backs of her naked legs.

The switchings were rare, for she had tried to be an exemplary child, never sassing adults or calling them by their given names. She'd washed and dried the dinner dishes without being asked and had never let a boy look under her skirt or touch where he shouldn't. And where had it gotten her? Marriage to the first man who'd asked, a child born in the first year of that marriage and desertion soon after Melanie turned two.

Bernice only allows herself to think of her phantom husband when she is sure Melanie is asleep. Only when she herself is covered up to her neck in blankets behind her closed door. Then she spreads her legs under the covers and watches the blankets sink into the deep indentation made by the space between her legs. She thinks of her husband—she still thinks of him as that—and the pleasure he used to make her feel before she knew it was all a lie. Lying like that, ensconced in deep memories and the touch of her own hands, it is easy to understand how a girl like Melanie could succumb.

Maybe she should go straight home. She hasn't given Melanie any notice. It is not fair, she thinks, to leave her daughter in a lurch. Then she remembers one Christmas, when they were watching *It's a Wonderful Life*, before Melanie outgrew her appreciation for the film. They'd been curled on the couch with hot chocolate and cream pie, watching as George Bailey ran up and down the one street in Bedford Falls, trying to convince the townsfolk that they knew him. Melanie had turned to Bernice and said, "That's what you do, right?"

"What, Melanie?"

"That."

Prim and priggish on the screen in a small tight hat and owlish glasses, a pinched woman Bernice hardly recognized as Donna Reed came out of the Bedford Falls Library and locked it for the night. Left to a life of loneliness without George Bailey to marry and rescue her, clutching her little bag and taking mincing steps, was Mary the town's librarian. Bernice tried to explain about InterLibrary Loan, high tech innovations and bustling activity. She tried to convince her daughter that being a librarian was not a last resort career for spinsters with nothing better to do, but all Melanie saw was a listless woman, idle and lonely, ensconcing herself in the consoling presence of books. Telling her otherwise had no effect on her. Once Melanie got an idea fixed in her head it stayed but good.

To hell with her, Bernice thinks, hanging up the phone.

She has always put her daughter first, always done what was best for Melanie, never what was best for herself.

Why not today?

Bernice sees herself approaching Harold and being witty, saying something like, "Forget lunch. Let's go straight to dessert," and offering herself to him, a slice of cake on a platter. She will wait until all of her work-study students are gone and she is the only one in the office. Wait until he is at the copier again. Step behind him, flick her tongue at the whorl of his ear. In no time at all her back will be against the copier, his hand—delicately—at the base of her spine, steadying…

…No, she could never do anything like that. Even in her fantasies, she cannot finish the thought.

Harold's voice, singing Blue Magic's "Sideshow," reaches her in the late afternoon.

He's singing the chorus when he walks past the ILL office. He stops when he sees her. "You still here?" he asks. He is without his mop, done for the day.

Bernice starts, as if from a deep sleep. She stares at the cartridges of microfiche on her desk, unable to remember if she has just pulled them out or if she is supposed to file them away. "I was just on my way out."

He steps inside. "I've never seen you leave so late before," he says. "You're usually in such a rush to get home. Guess you've got someone waiting for you."

Bernice rises mechanically, leaving the microfiche for tomorrow. "Just my daughter, who couldn't care less. What about you? Any children?"

"Grown and gone."

She shuts down her computer. "Lucky you."

"Yeah. Lucky. You know, I just want you to know I didn't mean any offense before. You know, that time when I asked you to lunch?"

"I didn't take it that way," she says, changing her shoes.

"No hard feelings?"

"Of course not." He pulls her coat from the peg and holds it out for her, as if he has always done so. She slides her arms through. "Harold, about that lunch?"

"What about it?"

"I'm free now, if you still want to go. We could make it dinner instead. What do you say?"

"Well, the thing is I can't."

"Can't?" she asks, momentarily nonplussed. "Today, you mean?"

"I've kind of met someone else."

"Else," Bernice says.

"I mean—I never thought you'd say yes. This woman—she's more my speed."

"Speed."

"You see, a woman like you and a man like me—I knew there was nothing there—I mean it wouldn't be what's best for you. I just thought I had to at least try. You didn't have to use the diet as an excuse. I understand, you know. You want to date somebody more your type. Somebody that's been to school."

"That had nothing to do with it," Bernice says. "I'm not like that." She doesn't know what she means by this, but it seems appropriately the thing to say.

"Everybody is like that," Harold says.

RESIDENT LOVER

SIX WEEKS into an artist's residency, Ray's wife wrote to say she would not be returning home. Ray took the news of the impending dissolution of his marriage like the gentleman he was. That is to say, he put his own feelings of hurt and anger aside and rationally tried to accept her decision, while determining his own part in it. He reasoned that it was likely his fault. He had, after all, encouraged her to stay the full eight weeks rather than opt for the two-week minimum. Two months was too long for anyone to be away, even in the best and strongest of marriages, which, admittedly, theirs had never been.

He should have seen it coming. His wife had accepted a two-month residency out in New Hampshire to complete her first book of poetry. At first, he'd gotten a few calls at night whenever the pay phone in the residence quarters was available. Then the calls began to come less frequently. After a month of silence, a letter arrived, stating that she had fallen in love with an installation artist from Delaware, a woman whose name was Djuna. She was declaring her separation from him. At the completion of the residency, she and Djuna were moving in together. She wanted nothing from him. She did not love him anymore.

He didn't write back.

All in all, he went on, careful not to let his inward turmoil appear on the surface. It can be said that he had occasional lapses. There were times when he forgot to brush his teeth and skipped his daily shave.

No changes, however, could be detected by the members of his department. He continued to meet with students. He agreed to direct the honors program. He appeared at all faculty functions alone, yet cheerful, seemingly unbothered by the solicitous questions about his wife. To the painful questions, he replied, "My wife and I separated this summer." He took care to imbue his response with dignity, to phrase it as a mutual parting between amicable parties.

Six months later, Ray was filling out his own application. At his keyboard, he typed in his full name, age, citizenship, present address, zip code and telephone number. Under permanent address he typed *same as above* and under email address he put *not applicable*. Though he wouldn't expect the organization to spam him, one could never be sure. The next line asked: *Please give the name, address and phone number of someone who can always reach you.* He decided against giving his wife's contact information. It was unlikely that he would have an accident during the residency, but in the case that he did, he knew she would not appreciate hearing about it. She would resent being held responsible. Inevitably, she would misconstrue his reasons for listing her and think it was his way of holding on. So he typed *I'm terribly sorry, but there is no one. No one at all.*

Finishing his application and going over it again, he stopped at his response to that question. It seemed stark, too revealing. More than enough to possibly have his application disqualified. The members of the selection committee would think he was gunning for sympathy. Or worse, that he was trying to be cutesie. But he could not change his answer. It was, after all, true. Would no one care if he broke his ankle on the other side of the country? Would no one be able to tell a doctor that he was allergic to penicillin if he came down with something? What had become of his life that the person who had been most close to him was now so estranged from him that she would not even wish to be bothered even if it meant it would save his life?

It was not the first time in his life that he cried.

When his father passed on, Ray had wept openly and unashamedly in the presence of his wife and the mourners who had come to offer condolences. He and his wife had been newly married then, just under a year, and like newlyweds they'd been so devoted to only each other that he'd failed to attend his father's deteriorating health. His father. The man who had coached him on how to deal with women. "Gentle, gentle," he'd once said by way of advice. He'd said it the way a doctor might soothingly say, "Steady, steady," as if love were a delicate surgical procedure through which one could be walked.

Beyond the passing of his father, Ray could remember no other time that he'd felt so desolate and alone. It didn't make any sense. The very act of writing for the application was meant to confirm that he was holding up, that everything was all right. If he were inconsolable, he wouldn't even be harboring such an idea at this point in time, would he? It was his way of moving on and putting everything behind him. He knew it was imitative at best, but he found he had no desire to be original.

He arrived late to the ranch, having flown from New York to Denver, where he then took a small commuter plane to Sheridan. The residency director held dinner back for his arrival. When he arrived, nine women—the seven residents, the program director, and the cook—arranged themselves at the dinner table so that he could sit at its head. The director identified everyone around the table by genre. There was one composer, one poet, one novelist, three painters and one printmaker. He was the only male in residence.

Over a hearty carrot and ginger soup and thick slices of homemade bread followed by angel food cake with a fresh fruit topping of brandy and glazed sugar, the women compared animal sightings of geese, sheep, and renegade cattle. Seated at a table set for dinner in autumn colors with matching linen napkins of hunter green, it was easy to see how his wife could have been seduced by the retreat environment, by the resident experience. Woven baskets lined the counters, full of fresh fruit, summer squash, zucchini and tomatoes from the garden. A ceramic cookie jar was kept filled with homemade biscotti. Near it stood an Indian spearhead which had been made into a tall candle holder. The decor was done to appeal to a woman's sensibilities. Everything was designed for ease and coziness. In the kitchen, the dish washing liquid smelled like tart green apples. At the dinner table, the salt sat in a small crystal dish with a tiny silver spoon. Two candles in lamp-like holders were placed on either side of a bowl of fresh cut flowers. The main house was decadent in its simplicity, designed to appear old-fashioned on the outside. A renovated school house constructed out of red-planked wood, it looked as if it had been built from one man's hands. The inside, however, was all modern, each room more lush than a hotel's.

While he was taking it all in, the woman to his right, a printmaker, brushed her hand against his leg too many times for it to be a mistake. The printmaker, Gianna, was overly made up, her eyes heavy with mascara, liner, and shadow. He wondered at the vanity of piling on makeup just to paint in isolation and was flattered to think that Gianna's mascara might have been applied with his arrival in mind.

The woman to his left—the prettier one—introduced herself as Felicia. "I work with watercolors and oils," she said, "Though not at the same time." Three of the women at the table laughed with her.

Before he could follow up with a question, Gianna turned to him. "Well, everyone else here gave their bio before you arrived. What's your story, Ray? Kids? How long have you been married?" Gianna asked.

"I'm sorry?"

"Married. You're married, right?" she asked, gesturing toward his ring.

"Not really."

Gianna invited him to come visit her studio and see her project. Ray nodded assent more out of politeness than genuine interest. What he wanted was to ask Felicia about the oils and watercolor comment. He sensed a closing in her when he failed to respond to her joke. He wanted her to tell him something else she thought was funny and give him a chance to redeem himself. When Felicia looked at him again, he saw her eyes were an unexpected color, a light almost clear green. Like celery, he thought. His wife once accused him of failing to pay attention to the things right in front of him. Celery was not good enough, Ray knew. If he absolutely had to describe Felicia's eyes, though of course he didn't, he would not say celery. He would say celadon. Or he would say that her eyes were like the first green shoots of spring, pliant and tender.

Ray lied down that night feeling optimistic. His surroundings made it hard not to feel like some sort of pasha in a harem. He was lying on a queen-sized bed with a plump red comforter and goldenrod sheets. Heavy draperies that swept the floor hung at each of his windows. An overstuffed couch was positioned near a large closet with sliding doors of weathered wood. In the closet were stacks of fuzzy velour blankets, a space heater, a flashlight, a can of bug spray and a fly swatter. His studio, which one of the guides showed him after dinner, was larger than he could have imagined, complete with a large granite-topped desk facing a wide window, a bookshelf stocked with reference guides, a futon, leather reclining chair and mini-refrigerator. He could live in his studio, sleep in his studio, if he chose. It was nestled in an area that promised serenity. Behind it ran a creek and sandy beach where he could pull his deck chair if he wanted. His lunch would be delivered to his studio every day. When he and his guide walked back from his studio, eighteen turkeys blocked their path as they crossed the dusty road just a few feet ahead of him. Ray advanced upon them, but they didn't startle. They kept their own pace until they had all crossed over to the grass where they pecked and pecked, their tiny heads and small red throats warbling.

Seven women, and just himself. He fell asleep to thoughts of them fighting over him, jockeying to sit near him at dinner, flirting coyly and sending him invitations to their studios. Though he had little admitted it before, it *had* occurred to him that such an opportunity as the residency would afford him not only the chance to finish the book project he needed in order to be promoted, but to meet women. He was taking a leaf out of his wife's book. If she could find love this way, then he could at least find companionship. The only other men here were part of the residence staff, the ones who kept the grounds. Bow-legged, weather-faced men with tough leathery necks, flannel shirts, jeans and hiking boots. The odds were in his favor. Tomorrow night he would dress for dinner in a sports coat, crisp white shirt, fresh slacks and cologne. He'd roll his sleeves to the elbow so the women would know that he could be both rugged and refined.

The program director joined them only when a new resident arrived. After that, no one saw her. Without her presence, everyone relaxed and shed their good behavior. Mostly, they swapped stories of previous residencies they'd attended. They told stories of much larger residencies which took up to fifty artists and writers at a time, and of ones tinier than this one, accommodating only five. They swapped stories of terrible residency experiences, of attending residencies that weren't really residencies at all, but odd setups in homes of the wealthy, of being asked to read or perform every evening like trained seals, of sharing spaces with residents who did not follow the quiet hours policy but chattered all day long and barged into other people's studios uninvited.

Unlike the others, Ray had no stories to share. He was the only residency virgin at the table. Each night he felt like an imposter sitting there amongst all of the women at the dinner table, but no one questioned him too closely about his writing project. One night at dinner during the second week, Felicia told the story of a poet at a residency in Illinois who had not understood the rules and who had made a nuisance of herself. She'd complete her work by ten AM every morning and dither the day away, pestering the others to keep her company and socialize. "If that wasn't bad enough, this was one of those residencies where we were 'invited' to present our work. We each got ten minutes or so, but she spent ten minutes just contextualizing and explaining what she was about to read before she even began. She pretended not to realize that the ten minutes were meant to cover both the reading time and the talking time. It was like she didn't understand the concept of time or believe that it applied to her," Felicia said. "She was the worst."

From the other end of the table, Gianna chimed in, "You think that's bad? Let me tell you—"

A week later, he came upon Felicia, sitting on the grass near his creek, trying to capture the landscape in watercolor. He'd been watching her from his studio, sitting Indian-fashioned on the grass as she alternated between staring into the distance and painting. From his window, she'd seemed serene and he'd thought she might talk to him out here by the creek.

He went to her. "It's beautiful, isn't it?"

"What?"

"Wyoming," he said.

"Wyoming is a whole state." She was close enough to him that he could see the freckles on her nose and cheek, nearly imperceptible on her brown skin.

"Yes, I know."

"Are you from the city?" she asked. She shielded her eyes to look up at him.

"I guess I am."

"Which one?"

"New York."

She nodded as if something had been confirmed. "Then this must take your breath away. It's so raw," she said. "So raw I can't capture it. Everyone tries to paint this."

He was of the opinion that one rolling hill looked pretty much the same as the next one, but he kept the thought to himself. His wife had once told him that he didn't look into things deeply enough, that he didn't interrogate life.

"How long are you staying?" He wanted to sit next to her, but she had a can of OFF and a plastic cup filled with water and paintbrushes at her side.

"I've got four more weeks," she said. She did not ask him in return, though he was hoping she would. He was on sabbatical, so he was staying for the full two months.

He rubbed the toe of his shoe deep into the grass. "If you do capture it before you leave, maybe you can show it to me in your studio some time," he said. She had already dismissed him and taken up her brush and miniature palette. Now she laid them both back in the grass and looked at him with interest.

"You an art buff?"

He said, "I know what I like."

He waited moments for her to say something. Finally, she picked up her brush again and adjusted the paper in her lap. "Sure," she said, with no real promise.

During the middle of Ray's fourth week on the ranch, it rained heavily. Although the weather had been warm and beautiful earlier in the day, by the time he'd made it in for dinner, he was soaked. Rain splattered the wooden deck and picnic tables in front of the building and pelted the windows while they all sat down to eat. The wind shook the trees and by the time they had all gone to their rooms for the night, the rain had become a storm sweeping the ranch.

Only a fool would be out in such terrible weather, yet he wondered if Felicia had dared to venture out into it. She appeared dutifully for dinner every evening, yet afterwards was nowhere to be found. Guiltily, he hoped her after-dinner disappearances had nothing to do with him. She'd been careful to avoid him in the days since he'd come upon her by the creek. He knew now that he'd asked her the wrong questions. The longer he remained, the more he understood the ways the artists spoke to one another. Being with them was almost like being a tourist in a foreign country. They spoke a language he did not understand. They talked about mediums and surfaces. Oil, pencil, charcoal, watercolor, acrylic. Paper, canvas, cloth, board, panel. They talked about the difference between 2-D and 3-D artists. 4-D they said, was a whole other thing. The painters identified everything by measurements, telling him something was twelve by twelve on cloth, six by six on canvas, tossing numbers and phrases like *acrylic wash on canvas* and *oil on paper* into the air at him at will. That afternoon by the creek, he had not known to talk to Felicia in this way. He'd blundered with her and he wanted a do-over, but he decided to take the hint. Residents were forbidden to visit each other's studios without express permission and he was not foolish enough to try to catch her at the creek again and embarrass himself further. More than once had his wife told him he lacked drive. She'd said that he gave up too easily, that he didn't fight for things, an accusation which he had denied at the time, but now suspected might be true. He could have worked harder to make their marriage smoother. Certainly, he could have pushed harder to get the department to do a joint partner hire. Although she was without a book, his wife's poetry had been published in literary journals. He could have negotiated with his chair and dean. They had wanted him badly enough. Yet he had held back. Quite honestly, though he had never voiced the opinion aloud, he had not thought his wife's material good enough for him to make the effort.

Sitting at the desk in his room, before the windows, he watched lightning crack the sky. He would not try to go to his studio the following day, guessing that the two mile trail would be seeped and muddy, impassable.

For three days straight the rain made it impossible for Ray to get to his studio. He worked from his bedroom during that time, missing the sight of mule-eared deer. He found Felicia in the kitchen on the third morning, complaining about bagels. "I do not believe this," he heard her say. She was alone, evidently talking to herself. She held an empty bag of Lender's Bagels in one hand and one bagel half in the other. "There's only one side of a bagel here. Who eats one side and leaves the other? Who else is going to eat it after someone's put her grubby hands all over it?" she complained.

She slapped the bagel half back into the plastic bag and turned to throw it into the trash. When she saw him watching her from the doorway, she glared. "It just seems so rude."

It could not be the bagel that was the problem. They met every evening for gourmet dinners, and their lunches were brought to them daily. It could not really be about the food in a place like this where food appeared from nowhere. Every time Ray looked for it, it was there. It waited outside his studio door at lunchtime. When he opened the door at noon, his lunch sat there in a basket. It waited for him at dinner. When he returned from his studio at night, it sat upon a table that had been set with him in mind. Breakfast was the only meal that was not provided, but no one could complain about something like that amongst the wealth of all the pampering the residency provided. Never before had he eaten so well. The first time he had opened the door to his studio and seen the neat little basket filled with exactly everything he wanted, he'd pictured his wife experiencing the same thing when she'd been in New Hampshire and thought *No wonder*.

Ray walked over to her and turned her hand palm side up. Together they looked at the dried paint beneath her nails. "Someone has been sneaking out in the rain," he tsked.

Felicia snatched her hand back. "No one said we couldn't use our studios."

"It's terrible out there. You shouldn't go alone."

"It's dying down. Don't worry. I'm a big girl and I have a big umbrella. I won't melt."

"I'll go with you."

"That's not necessary."

"You said you'd show me your studio some time."

She flicked on the switch and the room was flooded with light. Big halogen lights dominated the room. "I wish my studio had light like this," he said. "Then again, mine is much more comfortable." Her studio had no reclining chairs or footrests. There was a futon in the far corner near a sink and a large garbage can. The rest of the room was an assortment of tables made from slats of wood atop metal sawhorses. Ray stepped gingerly on a floor that seemed to be made entirely of drop cloth. "Is there anything beneath this?"

"Precautionary measures," she told him.

He pointed at all of the white paint. "Do you think you have enough?" he joked.

She smiled. "I go through more cans of white than anything else."

"What's this for?" he asked, holding up a can of hair spray that seemed out of place.

"Fixative," she said. "For when I draw in pencil."

"Right," he said, pretending to know.

"You said you weren't really married," she said. "But you're wearing a ring."

"We're separated." He followed her to the sink where she pulled off a wad of paper towels and tried to dry off her pants. He did the same.

"I'm sorry. Her decision or yours?" she asked. When he hesitated, she said, "You don't have to answer that."

"Have you ever been married?" he asked her.

"Yes." She tied on a smock splattered with paint. "How long have you and your wife been apart?"

"A little over a year now," he said. "She's a poet."

"Is she any good?"

"No. Not really," he admitted.

"Ever tell her that?"

"Not in so many words."

He'd told her with silence instead. Was that when it began to go badly for them, Ray wondered. Or had it been all the children? As if it were yesterday, he remembered when all of the children started coming. Out of the blue, they began popping up in her poems. Soon every poem she showed him was about some kind of child. He couldn't understand her need to focus on these smarmy children. They had no children themselves; his wife did not want them, did not even like them. She'd told him right from the beginning that she lacked the proper personality for parenthood, so why, then, had all of those children cropped up into her poetry, showing their grubby faces everywhere he turned?

He had not understood her weird children poems and when he didn't immediately shower her with praise for them, she held it against him, punishing him with abstinence. They were all so incomprehensible, so weird. Strange little poems about children. Dead children, children who died and spoke from the grave, children who went missing, who were orphaned, children in wheelchairs, children with leukemia, crippled children, boys who'd lost their dogs, girls who'd lost their pigtails, children who'd lost their teeth, their parents, their hair, their youth, their innocence, their lives—they were all little orphaned balls of sympathy; they were children meant to make one cry because the poetry itself could not. His wife's poems could not sneak up on anyone, could not get close enough to make one flinch and could never make a person shiver.

His wife's poems lacked the ability to touch the reader in any visceral way. He'd thought adding all of those children was a cheap trick on her part that weakened her poetry, a false tug at the reader's heartstrings. The children in her poems were clichés, shortcuts to sentiment. It was cowardly of her, he thought, to take the easy way out. Like everyone else, he had been a child himself and although he had not been an orphan, a cripple, or a cancer patient, his childhood had been hard enough. It had not needed anything extra other than the common pain of childhood— of wanting to be older than you were sooner than you ever could be, of feeling vulnerable and dependent, of waiting for everything, of being devalued—any and all of this was enough, hard enough, good enough for a slew of poems, he thought.

Felicia showed him around her studio. Pictures ripped out of magazines and hand drawings were taped to the walls above two of the tables. Her paint tubes, splattered and nearly flattened, lay all in a row in the middle of a table. Two of her studio's walls were covered in large sheets of canvas and the wall closest to the door was mounted with six panels. Extra panels were propped in a corner beneath a table. Felicia's artwork was surprising. Some of her paintings were done in various shades of gray and black. Other paintings had high chromas and their pure brightness made him happier than he ever remembered being. Long ago, he'd had to take an art history course in order to fulfill a humanities requirement for his undergraduate degree. In that course he had learned of chroma, value, and hue; he'd studied the way those three terms were used to express mood; he'd been taught the words and terms and meanings for what he saw, but until seeing Felicia's paintings the words had not become flesh.

"You've been here how many weeks?" he asked, failing to keep the wonder from his voice. He couldn't help but be impressed with her talent and her productivity. He hadn't expected her to have completed so much or for her paintings to be so good. Instinctively, he reached out to touch one, then caught himself and drew back his hand.

Felicia smiled at the compliment. "I like this kind of residency the best," she commented. "There are just a few people, just enough, you know? Just enough for company, to make you feel like you're not totally alone. The bigger ones can get out of hand."

"What do you mean?" He was surprised—happy—that she was finally talking to him this way. He guessed that being back in her studio and around her art relaxed her. He'd never seen her so open.

"They all start off the same. All everyone wants to talk about is what they're working on, what their craft means to them. And that's great because how often do you get to do that outside of a place like this? Most people aren't interested in those kinds of conversations. But somewhere around the midway point, that all flies out of the window and you start to notice that everyone is talking about personal stuff, everyone is just flirting. No more talk about craft. There are all of these inside jokes. It starts to become something like high school once again. Full of giggles. And that's the beginning of the end."

"You mean when the residency is almost over?"

"No, that's when it all becomes one big fuck fest."

"That happens a lot?"

She smiled condescendingly at him, as if she didn't really believe he was that naïve. "It's more noticeable at the larger residencies because there are more people there. You can't see it here because there's only you."

"My wife went to one of these things and never came back," he admitted. It eased him to know that this was something of a commonplace practice and it saddened him to learn that even in her affair, his wife had been derivative.

"What happened?" Felicia asked.

"She fell 'in love' with an installation artist," he said. "Or maybe it was more like lust."

Felicia looked sorry. "And you blame her," she said.

He did blame her, but he blamed himself a little too and being here gave him new perspective. Now, he could understand her in-fatuation a bit more. Here in this place of swift-running rivers, of slow-moving creeks, of unconcerned fowl, one could easily fall in love; in such a place it would be easy to misread the intellectual stimulation of being among your own kind for sexual fever. He was not even a real artist—not a painter, sculptor, novelist, poet, or composer, but even he could not deny the surge of energy that rushed through him after he completed a full day here of writing. He was not immune to that hot rush. It made him want to grab the nearest woman and kiss her soundly. It made him want to spend himself with someone. Even he, who'd fudged his scholarly project to make it sound more like creative nonfiction, while having no intention to really write upon the subject he'd proposed—even he got swept up in it all, in the uninterrupted hours between breakfast and lunch, between lunch and dinner, in the silence that emerged in the absence of television and work and worry and the distraction of real life, swept up in a current that made one believe that this was the only life and this life was the only one that held true.

Felicia propped her shoulder against the wall and stood watching him. She said, "You know, somehow I thought you would have visited me before this."

"You didn't invite me."

"I wasn't sure you had any taste. I figured you'd be too busy to make your way around to me with the way Gianna was fawning all over you."

"It wasn't that way," he said, careful not to mention that he'd al-ready been to Gianna's studio. He'd been unimpressed with its facto-ry-like setup, unimpressed with her forward nature and equally unim-pressed with her mediocre artwork.

"You're the only man at the residency," she said. "Of course it's that way."

"You're the one who let me come to your studio," he reminded her.

"You said you wanted to see it."

"I did," he said. "I wanted to watch you paint."

Felicia motioned him to the futon in the corner. "So watch."

Felicia chose a canvas that had already been covered in gesso to keep the oil paint from ruining it. He could see that she had already drawn on the canvas in pencil, but he couldn't make out what she was painting. From where he sat, he saw colors shimmering like a mosaic. What he could make out was the arch of her back, the delicate bones of her wrist, the way the hair at her temples became wavy and wet with perspiration. She seemed to stand without tiring; occasionally, she perched on something, but she never fully sat down. Ray offered to fetch her stool for her, but she waved him off, saying, "Real painters don't sit."

When pressed, she told him it was not good practice to sit while painting; she said it was better to use one's whole body. And she did. As he watched, Ray noticed that she used her full arm, and not just her wrist. "Only illustrators do that," she explained.

For a while Felicia talked him through much of what she was doing, but Ray eventually lost her. He called her name and she did not hear him, did not answer, lost in her process. Ray lost track of time watching her mixing paints, painting, and scraping paint, unable to tell whether he'd been in her studio for hours or for minutes. Soon, he no longer smelled the linseed oil and turpentine. Felicia painted tirelessly, only occasionally consulting the drawing tacked to the wall above it, never sparing him a glance. Felicia was gone from him, utterly absorbed in a way he could never be. He felt at peace there with her like that, with the music of the falling rain and the silence of no words.

He couldn't help himself. He fell asleep.

When Ray opened his eyes, Felicia was staring back at him, her eyes green and clear. She'd climbed onto him, straddling him with her knees.

"You were supposed to be watching," she accused. It was night outside her window. The rain had stopped.

"I'm sorry," he said. "I did watch, for a while."

"What did you see?"

He reached for her. Watching Felicia paint, Ray had witnessed true talent. He'd seen passion and dedication. "You," he said, unable to say more.

He'd witnessed his own shortcomings, seen his very lack. He had never—could never—give himself over so completely, but he wanted to feel that way, as if he could. He wanted to spread Felicia across him like gesso, to protect himself from ruin. He wanted Felicia to paint him, to include his face in one of her showings. He wanted to see himself in one of her gallery shows. Years from now, his face could wind up in someone's living room and make some couple happy. It could one day become a definition piece. Then—surely—his wife would see it and know what a mistake she had made in letting him go.

DIRECTORY ASSISTANCE

"IT's NOT like you're the first girl to fall in love, you know."

Somehow, Caroline's mother managed to sound both distracted and exasperated at once. Caroline could see her on her end of the phone, sitting in the study, creating financial plans for the lazy, the cordless phone wedged between shoulder and ear, wondering just how long this conversation with her wounded daughter was actually going to take.

"I do know," Caroline said, though in spite of her words, she truly did believe she was the only one to ever love like this, hurt like this. If there were others—her mother even—she did not care to know. She was enamored of the arrogance of her suffering, the sweeping way it swallowed all other feelings, washing them away like a monsoon.

"Just take a look at that girl Brad Pitt married."

"Jennifer Aniston?"

"Yes," her mother said. "Poor thing. The new guy dumped her too. She just can't catch a break. Even the rich white ones get their hearts broken."

"I really don't see what that has to do with anything," Caroline said. After all, she was neither rich nor white. She was a grad student, a girl who'd gone out to Northern California to earn her Ph.D. in English Literature because she loved books and didn't know what else to do with her life. Besides, everyone knew that celebrities didn't count.

"You can always come home," her mother said. "You don't owe them anything. There's nothing keeping you out there. Nothing but your pride. Nothing but yourself."

"If you think that's best," Caroline said, allowing her mother to think the whole thing her idea. Of course, she did not actually need permission to return home. There was plenty of room in her mother's four bedroom home in Overbrook Farms, near the Jesuit university. She did not need money; she had credit cards. She'd finished all of her course work and teaching requirements, so she didn't need permission from a dean, advisor, or graduate chair. She could simply "stop out," a euphemistic way of taking time off. Many had done it before her and some were now famous actors and golf champions. Pride alone had kept her out there. To leave of her own accord, without her mother's prodding, was akin to returning home with her tail between her legs. This way, if anyone asked, she could always say she had been needed at home.

Nothing could have been further from the truth.

Caroline was not needed at home—in fact—was too much underfoot, though her mother would never say it. Weeks after returning to Philadelphia, Caroline had called none of her old friends, having no desire to see anyone who knew her just now. "Pining" her mother called it. "Why are you always cooped up inside?" she asked late one afternoon after finding her ensconced on the living room couch with a light blanket and a bevy of snacks. "Go outside and get some fresh air." She snatched the blanket and shooed her outdoors like a child underfoot during summer vacation. "Come on and get out of this slump. Pining for him won't change a thing."

To appease her, Caroline caught the bus downtown to Center City. She got on just as people were getting off from work. All of the seats taken, Caroline held on to the strap and swayed with every turn the bus took, coming dangerously close to wounding the woman seated in front of her. With every curve and bump, Caroline's elbow threatened injury, but the seated woman remained unaware of the danger, absorbed in a book. Most of the seated women were all reading and all were equally consumed. Impossibly hampered for a day at work with unwieldy pocketbooks, packed lunches, and plastic bags to preserve their good shoes, these contented women in two-seaters were impervious to the pissy homeless riders behind them, the retarded, blind, and elderly riders in front of them and the noisy foul-mouthed youth crammed into the center aisles of the bus on either side of them. These women, with their hair pulled neatly back into fake buns, falls, or clumps of curls, their bodies bundled in bulky trench-like coats, their feet in gym sneakers, stretched their hands across the piles of bags in their laps and blithely turned the pages of books with the words *Scandal, Temptress, Captive,* and *Seduction* on the covers, ignoring all else on their way from work, completely absorbed, indifferent to the world around them until the driver announced their stop.

Caroline got off at her destination and went to *Robin's Bookstore.* There she stacked up on used romance novels selling four for five dollars. She chose the ones with discreet covers—a flower in bloom, or a woman's brooch on the cover—instead of a disheveled woman straining against her barely there bodice. On the ride home she began to read the illicit material, striving for kinship with the women she'd earlier observed, but her experience was not the same. *Perhaps,* she thought, *It is because I have nowhere to go.* She blamed her idleness for her failure to become engrossed. The other women had only the stolen minutes on the bus each day to read of medieval maidens with penchants for disguising themselves in men's clothing. Caroline had no such demands upon her time, and thus, no need to gorge. No one needed her anywhere at anytime to do anything for them.

Once Caroline accepted the position of Directory Assistant Operator for the telephone company some weeks after coming home, she was disappointed by the brevity of the ride. Assuming she'd work in the 17th Street facility where she'd taken the exam, she'd counted on a long and tedious bus ride to and from work, a ride that could make the pages of her novels fly by. The training office to which she was assigned was in Upper Darby, just a few blocks past the 69th Street Terminal, not far from her home at all. By bus, the ride took less than ten minutes, tops. As it was, the ten minute ride would not give her time enough to become absorbed in her books at all, but she had already accepted the job and they had tested her urine for drugs, so there was no help for it.

Dutifully, she arrived at the facility in Upper Darby, showing her ID to the old gray-haired woman at the front desk, taking the elevator to the third floor to train with the other DAs. She liked to refer to herself that way—as a DA—so that someone eavesdropping might mistake her for a district attorney. Not that she minded the term Directory Assistant; it was gender neutral, much nicer than Operator. It meant she was there to help, to provide vital information with impartial cordiality. Her former self might have looked down upon her new calling, but she had packed away the remnants of her old life and put it all behind her. Contrary to her mother's opinion, she was not pining, not nursing a broken heart, nor even thinking of *He Whom She Had Loved*.

That first day, a woman from Human Resources met with Caroline and the three other trainees to go over the paperwork and explain the phone company's dress code. Skirts and shorts (in warmer weather) were allowed, though women were to keep their knees covered at all times. Tee shirts were to be free of offensive designs or language. Tops with spaghetti straps were forbidden and at no time was the upper part of a woman's arm to be glimpsed.

"I feel like we've just stepped into the Middle East," a fellow trainee complained over lunch, after the HR rep was long gone. The young white girl wore a black tank top layered over a white undershirt and a flouncy patchwork skirt. In the microwave she heated a lunch that made the entire area smell like curry. The four trainees all ate their lunches in the lounge, a room cluttered with beat up couches that looked as though they had been picked up on sidewalk curbs by families who'd left them out to die. Directly behind each scavenged couch were large cardboard signs prohibiting employees from eating, napping, or putting their feet on the couches. Caroline skipped lunch in favor of her newest romance novel. She settled in on a lumpy couch and read.

"It's not that bad," another trainee, a much older woman, said, popping a pre-packaged frozen diet dinner into the microwave. "Dress codes instill respectability."

When the much older woman's back was turned, the only man in their group nudged Caroline and the white girl. "Take a good look at all of those pudgies out on the main floor," he whispered, taking his turn at the microwave and re-heating what looked like dinner left-overs. "Is it any wonder they want to keep everything covered up?"

The white girl laughed, but Caroline kept silent and continued to read about forbidden love between defiant Saxon women and for-midable Norman knights during the rein of William the Conqueror. The way she saw it, if she played her cards right, she need never show her bare knees again. *He Whom She Had Loved* had adored her knees. So free from the ashy buildup and the dark rough patches where the melanin was most concentrated. Caroline had her mother to thank for that. As a baby, her mother had limited her crawling.

The best DA's were brought in a half hour before the end of the first training day. Each of the six women told how many years they'd been with the company. None had been there less than five and many more had been there ten or fifteen. They all spoke warmly of the prizes at the end of the quarter for Customer Delight and Voice Appeal.

"I can't believe intelligent people work here," the white girl said under her breath halfway through the DA pep talk.

"What type of prizes?" the only male trainee asked.

"Good prizes," one of the younger women said. "Tee shirts. Jogging pants."

"Is the logo on them?" the white girl asked.

"Of course," one of the five DA's said.

"Sounds like free advertising to me," the white girl said.

"You've all been here so long, why haven't any of you become trainers or managers?" the much older woman asked.

An uncomfortable lull ensued, during which the six women all looked at one another without speaking. Finally, one of the DAs, Sarah, whined about the burdens of management, the on-call assignments, and the longer hours.

The white girl leaned over and whispered to Caroline, "They must have a good union here."

"What do you mean?" Caroline whispered back.

"They're union members. They don't want to cross over to Management and be scabs."

He Whom She Had Loved had been a big joiner. When Caroline met him, he was president of the Graduate Student Association and had been working campus wide to organize graduate fellows into a union to secure health benefits. Caroline had never understood the fuss. Joining the GSA and unionizing seemed to her just another way for doctoral students to focus on something other than finishing the program on time and prolonging their stay. When she failed to show his same enthusiasm, *He Whom She Had Loved* had called her selfish. He'd been disappointed by what he'd called her "lack of social consciousness and civic responsibility" when the truth of the matter was that she'd been having a hard enough time keeping up with her seminar papers, comprehensive exams, and trying to demonstrate her ability to read literature in two languages other than English.

Sarah stepped out of the room and came back with a man of average height wearing a headset. "We already have the best trainer around. We could never compete with Norman. All of the trainers actively take calls from the floor and Norman has the fastest time of anyone on the third floor. He averages five seconds per call," Sarah said, as though describing his time in track and field rather than phone operations. "It's a record."

Norman smiled and lifted his hand. For a moment, Caroline thought he might salute ala Tommie Smith and John Carlos at the Olympic games, but he merely waved and quickly seated himself at a large desk behind them. His blue-striped shirt strained across a soft belly and his dark brown pleated pants hiked near his crotch, turning his pants into high-waters, revealing fleshy ankles and sunken socks. His hair was a dull reddish brown that made his complexion ruddy. He struck Caroline as distinctly indistinct, so unlike *He Whom She Had Loved*.

"This is very challenging work," Norman said. At Caroline's involuntary frown, he flushed and said, "OK, it's not rocket science, but it takes a lot of practice to get everything down pat."

Soon after, they were released for the day. As they neared the elevator, the young white girl touched Caroline's arm. "You like this," she said. "I can tell. You're eating it up. You know they only hired us to get ready for their annual strike."

Caroline shrugged. "I'm just here to do something useful with my time."

The girl made a face. "Rocket science. That could be you in ten years."

When she deliberately said "you" and not "us," Caroline listened for a strain of something else in her voice. She was thinking too much about all of this, which was exactly what she no longer wanted. "I hope you're right," Caroline said, meaning it.

If she allowed herself to think, she'd have to remember that this year had been scheduled for work on her field proposal. Like those in her cohort, she had advanced to the stage where she would begin the research that would comprise her expertise in a field and be the starting point for her dissertation. If she allowed herself to think, she'd have to acknowledge that because of her relationship with *He Whom She Had Loved* and her own mediocrity as a fledgling scholar, she had accomplished nothing this year. Just now she pitied the cohort she had left. They took themselves too seriously, over-preparing for seminars, filling class discussions with so much theory that they ignored the primary texts, reworking seminar papers into conference talks, and taking forever to get out of the program in order to perfect their dissertations. She'd had enough of them and the things they held dear.

If she allowed herself to think, she'd have to admit that she had gambled and lost, pursuing graduate studies in a subject no one wanted to pay her for and for which she had no passion, pursuing a relationship with a man incapable of love. Those first few weeks back home, Caroline had stayed up all hours of the night, waking at the sound of the phone ringing, thinking it *He Whom She Had Loved*, though—logically—she knew it could not be. He didn't have her home number in Philadelphia, she had closed her university email account, and there was a three hour time difference to boot. Still, Caroline had lain awake for hours on those first lonely nights, hoping to hear from him.

If he could see her now, Caroline knew she'd have his pity. Her current situation would seem a step down to him, though she didn't see it that way. Just the other night, her mother had taken her out to dinner to congratulate her on getting a "real" job and, for the first time since the breakup, Caroline was starting to feel real again. She was no longer living off a stipend, forced to rely on her thoughts to provide for her. She had steady money coming in and the security that it would arrive every two weeks. She had not stepped down; she had stepped up into the real world where people had real problems and little time for idle thinking.

The next day, Norman took over their training. He had them sit at student desks with headphones and special keyboards while he walked around their small square of desks, individually handing each person a training guide. "This book should become the second most important book in your life, second only to the Bible. And even then it's a toss-up," he said, thumping the blue plastic three-ringed binder. "It's full of pertinent information. Chock full. Familiarize yourselves with it. Memorize the scripts. Read it when you're eating your lunches. Take it with you wherever you go. Sleep with it."

"I bet you do," the white girl mumbled under her breath.

Norman paused in front of Caroline's desk and looked back to where the white girl was sitting. He squinted at the girl and Caroline noticed the skin around his eyes behind his glasses was a paler brown than the rest of him. He rapped his knuckles against the binder. "Please turn to the section on Customer Delight."

At lunch, Caroline noticed that the only male trainee was now wearing a wedding ring. Since he'd obviously gone without it in the hopes of scoping out the prospects, its presence now made Caroline feel as though she'd been passed over, snubbed.

Norman entered the lounge five minutes before their lunch break ended and positioned himself next to the large digital clock mounted behind the TV. Caroline flipped back to her novel's cover, comparing the bare-chested warrior to Norman. Standing there with his hands on his hips, Norman was heroic, the protector of the phone company. He glanced down at the cover of her book, then picked up the training guide lying near her leg on the couch. "Why don't you try reading this instead?"

The young white girl failed to show up on the fifth day of training. One week later, the much older woman also vanished. Two weeks later, the lone male showed up two minutes late and was reprimanded for fifteen minutes. He was late twice more after that. In the middle of the fourth week, Caroline walked into the training room to discover herself alone with Norman.

"I'm proud of you for making it this far," he said, congratulating her as though she'd had something to do with getting rid of everyone else.

She'd thought it would be uncomfortable, just the two of them, but Norman went on as before. He taught as if the room was full, making use of the presentation board and avoiding eye contact. Caroline followed his lead and soon the awkwardness of being the only two people in a classroom faded as her head filled with Locality Codes, inputting, and Resident Extent of Search Flow Charts. They covered much more material without the others and spent less time having to role play customer scenarios. At home each night, Caroline pored over her binder, studying diligently, hoping to impress Norman the next day with her grasp of the material. "You're a fast learner. A real natural," he'd told her one afternoon, his voice as admiring as if he'd complimented her figure.

Two weeks later, Norman released her on the general floor for an hour to practice live calls. Sarah sat with her and listened in on the first few requests, giving her the thumbs up sign after each call.

A beep sounded in her ear. Caroline picked up the call, greeting the customer in her most courteous manner.

"You've got a nice voice," the man on the phone said. "It's very soothing."

"Thank you sir," she said.

"I bet you're cute," he said. "You must be a looker."

"Thank you sir."

"Are you?"

"Sir?"

"Cute. Are you cute?"

"I don't know, sir." Sarah shook her head and scribbled on a post-it note: *Key in Abusive Caller Code and Disconnect.*

"What are you wearing little lady?" the man asked.

"Is there a listing I can find for you sir?" Caroline asked, trying to salvage the call.

The dial tone rang in her ears, amplified by the closeness of the small headset.

"We get a few of those a day," Sarah said.

Caroline pulled off the headset. "Pervert," she said. "Sicko."

"Just lonely." Sarah keyed in the abusive caller code and motioned for Caroline to put her headset back on. "We're a lot cheaper than phone sex."

Caroline told Norman about the caller over lunch. They'd walked to the United Artists movie theater to eat in its Food Court. They had taken to eating their lunch together every day now that Caroline was the only remaining trainee.

Norman carefully unwrapped his chicken sandwich and took a huge bite. "The old man was getting his jollies, eh? Thought you were cute?"

"I didn't say he was old."

"'Course he was. Nobody our age would be into that," Norman said. "Our generation doesn't feel that type of alienation. And if we do, we know what to do about it." He attacked his fries, putting five into his mouth at once.

"Which is?" Caroline asked, too polite to point out that she and Norman did not belong to the same generation.

"We've got the Internet. No one has to be alone, if they don't want to."

She was unsure if he was referring to Internet dating or cyber-porn, and did not want to know. She pretended not to notice his bad grammar, ignoring the awful way he'd mixed singular and plural, following 'no one' with 'they' instead of 'he' or 'she'. "Have you seen any of these?"

Norman scanned the release posters briefly. "Nope." He took another bite and his eyes drifted closed as he chewed. "So, you want to catch a flick some time?"

She had not meant to suggest a date. "I was just wondering if there was anything worth seeing."

"We can find out together," Norman said.

"No, really."

"Okay, dinner then? I'll cook," Norman said. "I know my way around a kitchen. What do you say?"

He Whom She Had Loved had never offered to cook for her. "If you insist."

Norman squinted at her behind his glasses and lowered his chicken sandwich. "Hey. Know something?"

"What?"

"You are kind of cute," he said, as if just noticing.

Caroline followed three blocks of duplexes before she finally found Norman's. The University City homes were different from the ones in Overbrook—sprawling mansion-like houses, cut and dissected into apartment units, and rented out at exorbitant prices to Penn undergrads. Norman lived near an arcade.

He opened the door in a blue cotton apron embossed with the phone company's logo. On his feet, he wore slippers that bore the company's logo as well.

"Find everything okay?" he asked. He attempted to greet her with a kiss, but Caroline turned to give him her cheek and he ended up kissing the side of her nose wetly.

"Sorry."

"My fault." Norman cupped her shoulders to hold her still and kissed her on the lips. "Glad you could make it."

"Me too," she said, unsure if she liked him kissing her. She had accepted his invitation, but she had not thought beyond that, and now wondered if she had given him the wrong impression.

Norman ushered her past a sparsely furnished living room. He had no coffee table. His couch, black leather, was flanked by two glass end tables covered with mail. A flat paneled television dominated the wall opposite the couch. He took her jacket and hung it in the small closet by the stairs. He swung the closet door too wide and Caroline stumbled backwards over two metal push up bars sprouting from the floor.

Norman picked up the bars and dumped them in the closet. He touched his stomach self-consciously. "I've been meaning to get around to using them."

Caroline couldn't picture Norman doing even one pushup, could not imagine him exercising at all, could not even begin to think of him without his shirt. She could only see him in the office, managing the unit. There, in the training room, Norman seemed heroic, larger than life. He seemed born to work for the telephone company. He was adept at explaining how to get to the different screens for residential and business numbers, yet outside of the small training room, he shrank back down to size and hardly merited notice.

"Dinner's about ready. I'll bring it out."

"May I help?"

"Just have a seat," Norman said, disappearing under the arch of the dining room.

Caroline sat back on the leather couch and looked around Norman's empty living room. The absence of a coffee table made the living room appear larger. Why did Norman have so much mail, she wondered, looking at the haphazard stacks of it on the end tables. She fanned out one stack and found several glossy magazines mixed in. Black women, dressed in bikinis or bras and thongs, squatting with their bottoms facing the camera while they looked back over their shoulders, peered back at her. She slid the magazines under Norman's bills. She remembered the day he'd criticized her romance novel and wondered now how he could have dared when he owned such smut.

Norman came into the living room holding a roasting pan. "Cornish hens."

Caroline rose from the couch. "Should I follow you to the dining room?"

"Actually, I didn't have time to clear off the table in there. The birds took longer than I expected. Mind if we eat in here?" Norman asked. "There are some TV trays in the closet. Can you grab them?"

Standing there, with his Cornish hens held high in a white-speckled blue roasting pan between his two oven mitt-clad hands, with his blue apron belted tightly across his stomach, Norman did not seem like the type to gorge himself on centerfolds. Just now, he seemed nervously intent upon pleasing her and she found his awkwardness endearing. *He Whom She Had Loved* would not have cared if his dining room table were clean. He would have merely pushed the books and papers to one side, expecting her to eat among the clutter.
After dinner, Norman led her upstairs.

"Want to hear anything in particular?" he asked, handing her a zippered case of CDs. While she flipped through his music, he began to rub her arms. When he'd made it up her arms, he lightly brushed the sides of her breasts with his knuckles and leaned his mouth into hers.

It wasn't real to her until Norman began to undress. He removed his shirt, revealing a body that was fleshy, soft in places where it shouldn't be. She had no desire to look at his nakedness. Instead, she closed her eyes and thought of Norman in the training room, so focused on the material that he never glanced her way. She thought of Norman at their lunches, his eyes riveted to his meal, his mouth chewing with relish. As he removed more clothing, he became less and less the forceful Directory Assistance trainer and more and more the pitiful man. The same kinky sandy-colored hair that was on his head dotted Norman's chest and stomach, making him look rusty. Norman couldn't make her hunger, she knew. He was incapable of driving her clear across the country just to escape the possibility that, in a weak moment, she might relent. No, she wouldn't have those worries with Norman. He'd be grateful to have her; he would appreciate her. Even as Norman pushed her back against the bed and prodded clumsily against her, Caroline felt herself completely safe, impermeable.

The last time they'd made love, *He Whom She Had Loved* had placed his hands on either side of her face, holding her so that she could not get away.

Trapped by his torso, pinned by his pelvis, imprisoned by his palms, she could do nothing but look straight at him. "I'm serious," he'd said. "I'm telling you what I've been telling you all along and I am serious. I do not want children." He'd still been inside of her when he'd said it, still turgid, still ensheathed. He'd been using condoms for the last few months, saying he did not trust her not to take things into her own hands, but that night he had forgotten and she had not reminded him.

She'd had no words. Just a minute ago, he'd been thrusting inside of her, sweating with passion and capable only of the most guttural of sounds. Now he spoke as if they were sitting at a table having coffee. She was still holding him within her, still distracted by passion. She could not answer, could not begin to summon a coherent thought.

"Do you understand me?" he'd asked her, his palms pressing, covering the flesh between ears and chin.

He waited for her to nod. Instead she'd turned her face and licked his palm.

A look she did not know, had never before seen and could not decipher had then come over his face. He'd torn himself away from her, pumped himself into his hand, and spilled himself across her stomach.

After that they spent no more nights together. She was not invited over. She was not called. She was not run into on campus. She was forgotten and ignored. Months later, she was not taken to the airport when she left the Bay Area. She was not bidden farewell. She was not seen off.

It wasn't even that she'd wanted to have children just then. She'd merely mentioned that one of the benefits of an academic life was that faculty members received tuition remission for their dependents and that, once factored into an academic's salary, the money the university paid out in that manner made the pay more lucrative than it initially appeared.

"That's only a benefit if you actually want children," *He Whom She Had Loved* had said. "I don't want any."

"Not right now, of course," she'd said. "Nobody wants kids while struggling to make it through grad school."

"No," he'd said. "Never. Not after grad school either. Not now. Not later. Never."

They'd been in the student center at Tresidder Union, at one of the tables downstairs, an umbrella between them to shield them from the sun. He'd gone back to eating his naked burrito, but eventually had looked up again. There must have been something in her face, but she couldn't know what he was seeing. "You want them?" he'd asked.

"I don't know if I do," she'd said. She took a sip of the smoothie she'd purchased at the Jamba Juice, trying to taste the bee pollen infusion. "But I don't know that I don't." They were used to talking like this, making fine distinctions. Being unsure as to whether one wanted children was not the same thing as not wanting children. Being attracted to a person did not necessarily make the person attractive. Being willing to eat was not the same thing as being hungry. He'd accused her then of being evasive. This time, he'd said, it was different. She either did or did not want children. He'd behaved as if she had not only said that she wanted children, but that she wanted them as soon as possible and that she wanted him to be their father. He began to bring it up whenever she came over and they made love, ruining the post-coital splendor with talk of the children he did not want and she did or did not know if she wanted. There had never even been a baby. Neither real, nor rhetorical. The child—literal, figurative, metaphorical, physical, wanted, unwanted—lay between them each time they made love and his words, which she had originally taken as purely intellectual musing began to strike her as deeply personal, as if he were rejecting her as a future mother, as if he were saying not that he didn't want children, but that he didn't want them with *her*.

Norman nudged her awake with his leg. "Are you asleep?"

"What is it?"

Norman shifted under the covers, propped himself on an elbow to face her. "I've been thinking about tonight and I just want you to know that things between us will have to change once the strike hits. On the surface, that is."

"What strike?" she asked, though she knew. She had eyes, after all. In the past two weeks, she had seen two new training classes begin. Though the company could not purposely hire people who would not strike, it could count on most newer hires to be loyal to their paychecks rather than to the union, and hope that the trainees' fear of losing their jobs would convince them to cross the line.

"Don't be coy."

"Change how?"

"We'll have to face off each day, but—just remember—when the day is over, we can always come back to this," Norman said, as if offering incentive.

"Why are you saying this?"

"The long hours I work make it hard for me to get out a lot. Most of the women I've been with have come from inside the company." Norman ran a finger up her bare arm and said, "Let's just say that relationships become strained when two people are on opposite sides of the line."

"So you dated a woman a while ago and then the two of you broke up because of the strike?" Caroline asked, unable to picture Norman as a Lothario with his pick of the company's women.

"I've lost *a lot* of women that way," Norman said. He rolled away from her and lazily propped his hands behind his head. "Hey, why don't you get me some water?"

"Why can't you?"

"You're closer," he said, though, in truth, she was not.

In Norman's bathroom, Caroline pulled a small paper cup from the dispenser near his toothbrush holder and filled it with cold tap water, thinking of this thing that could come between them. When she had been ensconced in the world of academia with *He Whom She Had Loved*, she had thought little of the outside world and its every day functions. In her present life, the mundane workings of daily life had come to mean a great deal to her so that she now cared deeply about health care benefits, sick days, paid leaves, vacations, and raises.

How lightly Norman had spoken of past women. How blithely he'd expected to be waited upon.

She imagined the two of them on opposite sides of the line, she with the union strikers and Norman with the managers and scabs. All day, she'd stand outside the building, holding a sign, powerful in her red shirt, part of a unified wall of bodies seeking better wages and more job security. She'd see Norman going in and out of the building in the morning and at lunch with the scabs. Unlike the other managers who would at least pretend to look guilty as they passed the strike line, Norman would be unperturbed. He'd walk past with his head held high, refusing to scurry or duck. He wouldn't quicken his pace. He'd stride past the strike line and when the strikers threw insults at him, he'd turn and face the crowd, squinting at the catcallers. When he saw her, he'd raise his hand briefly—unconsciously—as if to wave, then drop it quickly before anyone saw. Without a backwards glance, he'd cross the line and join the other managers, dividing the two of them but for a moment of involuntary recognition.

CICERO WAITING

How can he think of anything but the devastation of Pompeii, the prosperous town covered in twenty feet of white ash when he stands before the fifteen students in his eleven o'clock class? His students are earnest and young, with fresh open New England faces. A large majority of them are townies. Most of the boarders are from Keene, Brattleboro, Worcester, Northampton. They are in his class not because they bear any love for Classics, but because they think it is easy. Latin is the only language that does not come with a listening exam. When they enter his classroom, they pause and say, "Salve magister." The boys remove their caps without being asked and the girls cross their legs at the knee. He couldn't ask for more. So how can he forget the lesson about that August morning in A.D. 79, especially when he has already begun to list words for the night's translation on the board:

L.	*Engl.*
cinis	*ash*
exanimatus	*unconscious*
atra	*black*
fumum	*smoke*
pavor	*panic*
flammae	*flames*

ruinas	*wreckage*
exspiravit	*died*
moribundus	*almost dead*

Only the last two words need explanation. He is lecturing on the shades of difference in Latin vocabulary and grammar, cautioning the students to seek the most precise translation and explaining when to use *moribundus* in place of *exspiravit* when he sees her. Looking over the tops of his students' heads and out the room's one window onto the campus, ignoring the students outside hard at work on their makeshift apple press, he sees two administrators leaving Kittredge early. The two women, dressed in low heels and drab suits are making their way up the winding path from the bottom of the hill. One of them is his wife. He forgets what he is saying when he sees her, hatless and coatless in the brisk cold of late autumn. He can't tell yet if she will turn off the path and go home for lunch, or if she will continue on to the dining hall or if she will come to him. Last week, she had stopped in the Classics building at lunch time when he wasn't expecting her. She'd caught him by surprise, dragged him to the dining hall and made him eat with her. It wasn't something he wanted to repeat. When he turned his attention back to his students, they were right where he left them, patiently waiting with pencils poised. He had no idea how long he had been staring. He thought of dismissing his class early so he could gather his things and find a place to hide. The bell rang then, preventing him.

He went to his office and stuffed a stack of *Somnium Scipionis* translations into his attaché. The leather was worn, the handle loose and tricky. His wife had given it to him during his first year of grad school at Stanford. Back when he'd had aspirations to be a professor and wouldn't have considered teaching at his old secondary school. As he snapped the lock, the phone rang in his office. He answered it automatically.

"Classics Department," he said, even though the department consisted only of himself and one other teacher who taught Greek.

It was his wife. "Are you hard at work?" she asked.

"I'm preparing for my next class," he lied.

"It's lunch time," she said. "Aren't you going to go to the dining hall? I can meet you there."

"I really don't have the time. I've got a lot to do."

She sighed. "Who is it this time? Ovid? Martial?"

"Cicero," he said. "*Somnium Scipionis.*"

"Well how about I just bring something to you, then? There's still a lot left over from last night."

"No, but thanks. I'm going to work through lunch. I probably won't have time to eat," he said.

He heard her sigh. She paused longer than necessary before she spoke again. "All right, but don't work too hard. We're on duty tonight. From dinner until dorm closing," she said. "I love you." She hung up without waiting for him to respond.

He was teaching pronouns to his next class. To prepare for it, he went back to his classroom and wrote out the masculine, feminine and neuter singular forms of the relative pronoun qui on his green and dusty chalkboard:

	M.	*F.*	*N.*
Nominative:	qui	quae	quod
Genitive:	cuius	cuius	cuius
Dative:	cui	cui	cui
Accusative:	quem	quam	quod
Ablative:	quo	qua	quo

He would call his students up, one by one, and have them supply the different plural endings. The next class would be his fourth of the day and he would coast, teach by rote, counting off the minutes until the bells tolled and finally freed him after eighth period. He would venture out during one of the bells when it was safe. There were ten minutes between them. Enough time for him to run to the student snack bar and order a grilled cheese with tomato to hold him over. For now he would stay put.

He walked to the window and opened it slightly, enough to let in the smell of the school. The school took on a different scent depending on the season. The air smelled sticky and sweet when the apple cider press was going full steam in the fall. He loved the smell of maple syrup slowly being tapped from the trees in the winter and in the spring, there was the scent of dewy freshly cut grass in the mornings. These scents had comforted him as a fourteen-year-old fresh from the city. As a freshman, he used to keep his window open in all seasons. It made him feel closer to nature in some way, as if the seasons were living and breathing through him.

Students piled onto the buses for the away game. Workers in blue pull-overs with the school's logo stitched above their hearts blew fallen flame-colored leaves and collected them into careful piles. He had a clear view to the path of maple trees that lined the way to the administrative buildings. Past the path and near the farm, he could smell the fresh manure and yesterday's leaves burning in the open air. Beyond the trees was the wide open football field, then the gym and the Connecticut River, peaceful and serene. When he and his wife first moved to the campus, they used to take long walks down to the boat house and the docks and watch the water. When he was down there with her hand in his, he blocked out the nuclear plant across the river, and focused on the deceptive surface of the icy water. In the morning, the crew team owned that space, stocky men and women carrying their boats above their heads, rowing on the Connecticut in preparation for the races at the Head of the Charles. The campus was quiet at this time of the day. Quiet moments like these unnerved him, their peaceful tranquility merely an illusion. He felt a promise of peace he couldn't trust when he looked out among the freshly manicured grounds of the campus. The Pompeians had been warned. It rained hard the night before the eruption. The earth quaked and storm winds blew. Mud poured out of the mountain and covered the town of Herculaneum, but only a few in Pompeii paid heed and fled. Most waited too long, thinking the violent storm would pass. No doubt the twenty thousand inhabitants on the coast of the Bay of Naples at the foot of Mount Vesuvius had felt that same promise right before the sleeping volcano awakened and rained hot stone and ash down upon them, burying them where they stood.

He didn't know until it happened that little girls could go lost.

Nine months ago, he'd lost his three year old daughter in Target. He and his wife were living in Palo Alto while he worked towards his Ph.D. at Stanford. They had a perfect setup. She had a job on campus in the financial aid office and he kept an eye on their daughter while he worked on finishing his dissertation at home. They lived in housing set aside for graduate students, a section of Stanford's campus devoted to hi-rises and small brown houses. They had two bedrooms, a kitchen, bathroom and living area. The second room doubled as his daughter's room and his study.

He'd been working on translating a particularly difficult passage for several weeks and it showed. The laundry was piled over the hamper and their voice mail was full. It was winter quarter and his wife was swamped at work with FAFSAs and creating financial aid packages. Proud of himself for nailing the translation, he'd decided to carry his sense of accomplishment further. He packed their daughter into the car and went to Target to buy detergent. He would help out by doing the laundry. It would be a surprise for his wife.

It pained him to think of how easy it had been to lose his daughter. One minute, she was near him, playing among a nearby rack of clothing, her head dwarfed by two-pieces on hangers, her feet visible.

The next minute she wasn't there. He turned around to drop the econ-
omy-sized liquid detergent into his cart and she was gone.

Ten weeks later, the police found his daughter's body.

He couldn't stay in California after that, he had no desire to finish
his dissertation and warm temperate weather and blond brick buildings only seemed to mock him. He did not inform his graduate chair;
he didn't consult his wife. He called the Alumni Relations office at his
old prep school and asked if they had any teaching positions open in
Classics. Deciding not to finish his dissertation was self-inflicted pun-
ishment; he didn't feel he deserved a doctorate after that.

It didn't take much for him to remember. The sight of his wife was
enough to trigger him. It would be easier for him if he could leave her,
but an unspoken code prevented him. After all, he was the one at fault.
He didn't have the right; it was up to her to do the leaving.

If he called her back, he could catch his wife before she finished her
lunch and headed back down the hill. He wanted to put an end to this.
To tell her to just leave. To say that he is tired of waking up each day
wondering if it will be the one where she finally understands what he
has done. He wanted her to stop trying to pretend to make things work
out somehow when they both knew it wasn't possible. She was selfish,
cruel to tease him this way. Didn't she understand how difficult it was
to stay away from her? How hard it was to concentrate on Cicero and
Catullus and Vergil, knowing that any day she could pack and leave?
Did she know the students were used to him blanking out in class?
Strange how he could be listening to a student recite and look out the
window and catch sight of a girl with his daughter's walk, her funny
clumsy pigeon-toed way of walking with her feet overlapping. He had
refused the doctor's suggestion that they break his daughter's feet to
re-set her bones. He had thought the way she walked was cute and he
couldn't bear the thought of her legs in braces. Every now and then he
would see a girl walking up the hill towards the dining hall and her odd
way of walking would arrest him.

If his wife would listen, he would tell her all of that. But if he only had time to say one thing before she hung up, he would let his wife know how hard it was to look at her. Each time he did he saw their little girl. Not at the age she had been when she was taken, but at the different stages in her life not to come. In his wife's eyes he saw her growing, maturing, developing into a woman, saw her in the familiar contours and planes of his wife's cheeks and neck and throat, and on the surface of her brown skin. When his wife held her arms out to him as she sometimes did when she couldn't help it anymore because the pain was just then too great for her and she knew that it was always too much too much for him and so she couldn't help but to supplicate and try and find a way out of it through the comfort of each other's arms and so reaching for him to pull her in and not let her fly away to the places where the memories were taking her and she lifted her arms and beckoned or beseeched, he never knew which they were, the arms of his little girl clamoring to be lifted up and swung high in the air, a plea he could not deny the little girl who knew it, or the arms of the woman who wanted to be held and comforted.

She believed that they could heal. She wanted him to help her get through this, but he couldn't even help himself. He didn't want her to forgive him. He didn't want them to be strong. He didn't want to excavate and rebuild. Those who had fled Pompeii and survived returned the next day to find their city buried. They dug tunnels to get down to their houses in order to salvage what valuables they could. But the town could not be rebuilt. Pompeii couldn't be saved. The city had to be abandoned. The ruins gradually collapsed and Pompeii disappeared, the site of the town lost under a new layer of soil. If only he could make her listen and understand.

"Is that the last of them?" he asked his wife. "It's almost eight."

His wife stood hunched over the sign-out book, a simple black binder that logged the nightly comings and goings. Just then, in her faded gray sweats and her hair looped into a ponytail with the ends tucked up and under, standing with her back to him, slightly slouching, she could have been one of the students, one of the boarders signing herself out to study in the library, or to use the language labs or meet with a study group. She could have been anybody then, anybody but his wife. Had she been anyone else, he could have gone to her.

"That's everybody," she said. "Wait. Didn't Vesna bring a boy in?"

"I think so."

"She never signed him in."

"I'll check and make sure he's out." He was already mounting the stairs, glad to have something to do.

"Room 314," she called after him.

Girls clamored down the stairs as he made his way up, barely noticing him, as they ran down the stairs with their heavy one-shouldered bags and rushed off for their last two hours of freedom before he locked the dorm for the night.

He knew what room Vesna was in. She was a black-haired girl from one of the tiny warring countries in Eastern Europe. She had a habit of sneaking in boys and burning incense in spite of the school's fire hazard code.

Her door was closed. He hoped for her sake that the boy was gone. Otherwise she'd be in violation of the Visiting Hours policy. The door was to be kept open and the room fully illuminated when a person of the opposite sex visited.

He knocked.

Vesna answered the door in a tank top and plaid boxers, holding a bag of French Onion Sun Chips. "Hey," she said.

"You never signed your Visiting Hours guest in." He peered into her room. A blue scarf was draped over the bulb of her desk lamp, giving the room a nightclub feel, making it hard to see if anyone else was inside.

"Oh. Sorry."

"Mind if I come in?"

She shrugged and opened the door wider.

"Where's Machiko?" he asked as he circled the tiny room, not seeing anything worth noting. The closets had no doors and the beds were too low to the ground to hide a person.

"I don't know. Play rehearsal probably."

Vesna sat on the bed, eating her chips, watching him. He couldn't catch her this time, but he didn't want to leave empty-handed. He pointed to the scarf. "You know that's a fire hazard."

"I forgot." She wiped crumbs off her bare legs. She didn't bother to remove the scarf.

He was disappointed Vesna had been alone. Most likely, Study Hall would be just as uneventful. He liked it when there was a dorm emergency, when some student was missing after Lights Out, or when they caught a boy sneaking out long after he should have been gone.

He went back down to the second floor and gave his wife the go-ahead to ring the bell to start Study Hall. He grabbed his leather bag and took it with him down to the Study Hall room.

These were the things he was supposed to do as a Dorm Parent: Restrict any student he caught using the dorm elevator, which was reserved only for faculty. Meet weekly with his Student Leaders. Conduct room inspection once a week. Plan a monthly House Meeting complete with snacks. Meet with dorm faculty. Take his turn covering the two hour supervised Study Hall for the kids on academic probation. He liked his duties. He wanted to stay buried here in this area where the towns were named for fields: Northfield, Greenfield, Springfield, Deerfield. Here on this wide campus. Here in this dormitory housing that was constantly bustling with the vain and needful wishes of adolescents who believed it was his job to be always on call and available to them, who entered his home unannounced and expected snacks and drinks as well as advice, yet who would think nothing of leaving him during the midwinter recesses and longer holiday breaks, who would never come back to visit after graduation. They wanted recommendations for college. They wanted a safe place to cry. They wanted him to take away their horrible roommates and switch them for perfect ones, and he wanted to lose himself in their worries until there was no room left for his own.

At ten thirty, he locked the dorm's double doors for the night. Then he went upstairs to make sure the Student Leaders had checked all the freshmen in for Lights Out. By the time he got to his own apartment off the second floor, his wife had showered and settled in for the night.

"Was everything okay? Any problems?"

"Not tonight." He kicked off his shoes and left them in the living room.

"Did you lock the front doors downstairs?"

"Yep." He went to the kitchen and grabbed a beer to take to his study.

"I think that Vesna's a slick one."

"Undoubtedly."

"That boy will probably be back tonight."

"That's a possibility." He turned on the lamp in his study. He set down the beer on his desk and dropped the half-zippered bag onto his chair. The students' translations of Cicero fell out. He had a long night ahead of him. He didn't get anything done today in his office. Hopefully, by the time he finished his grading, his wife would be fast asleep.

"Sure you locked it?"

"Nice and tight."

"Come here, please."

He made his way from the study to the bedroom and stood in the doorway.

She was wearing that special lotion of hers again, he could smell it from the doorway. It made him want to go to her. He had bought it for her on Valentine's day a few years ago. The lotion had been part of a set. It came with shower gel, bath bubbles, bath salts and some sort of loofah. He used to let her shower first just so he could linger in the scent she'd left behind. The gel had been finished off quickly. The lotion should have been as well, but somehow she always managed to squeeze out one more drop, refusing to give up without a fight. That lotion made her smell like part garden, part Heaven.

"Are you coming to bed?" his wife asked.

He stood like a bridegroom in the door, staring at her, seeing her for perhaps the first time since they'd lost their little girl, seeing her face and the beauty of it in the soft down of her cheeks.

"Not yet," he said. He knew how it would be if he walked fully into that room. She would be there, sitting up in the middle of the bed on the left side, her dark hair rumpled against the headboard. In a white nightgown, her face scrubbed clean but not glowing. Her knees would make a tent under the sheets and if he got in, she would shock him with her cold feet. If he came in the room, she would hold out her arms and once again it would be a struggle not to go to her and let her help him make a way to be more than he had become. But he knew that if he let her hold him in her arms that he might never want her to let go again, never rise from the bed and teach another participle, never leave the sanctity of her. Then what would become of his Latin, his students' translations of *Somnium Scipionis* lying face-up on the floor of his study?

"More work?"

"Cicero—a stack of papers—they're waiting for me."

"I'm waiting for you."

"I need to finish them."

She patted the empty side of the bed and held out her arms to him again.

"I promised to hand them back tomorrow."

He swallowed, wondering why he felt as if he were in one of those dreams everyone had where they fell endlessly.

She said nothing, but her eyes were leveled on him. She waited for him to decide.

"Honey, I can't," he said.

"Yes you can."

He took a step towards her and stopped just within the doorway. During the nights with her asleep beside him, he clung to the idea of maples and pines, of students who should have kept him too busy to think of anything but the next day's lesson. But there were these unbearable moments that seemed longer than they could possibly be; they seemed to come from nowhere and hold him captive. "I don't know what to do."

"Come here," she said. "I'll show you." Could it be that simple? Her arms, her eyes said yes. It would be the first time, since the school year began, that he didn't grade translations late into the night. He could let them wait. They would be there tomorrow, but this night might never come again.

A BRIEF PAUSE

THREE WEEKS after Roger's mother dies, we are having breakfast in our kitchen. Our table is cluttered with my stacks of admissions files for the college's incoming transfer students, so we pull our chairs up to the kitchen island and eat around large mixing bowls, hunching to keep from being beaned by the unused gleaming copper pots hanging just above our heads.

Roger has made this breakfast, though it is my turn, and he has made more than we can possibly eat. English muffins, blueberry waffles, scrambled eggs, turkey bacon, and freshly brewed coffee—much more than the two bowls of cereal and two glasses of orange juice I usually pour. I am choosing between an array of fruit preserves—strawberry, red raspberry, blackberry, boysenberry—when Roger asks me to drive with him over to Brooklyn to help clear out his mother's apartment.

His face carefully hidden behind the Sunday paper, he pretends innocence when he asks, knowing this is not our arrangement. Behind me, on the kitchen table, lie the academic lives of prospective students. Hopeful and striving, after one or two years at their current institutions, they have decided that they can and should aim higher. Perfect and nearly perfect GPAs prove they are up for the challenge. Candid essays ask me to rescue them, to extricate them from their current schools—schools that were their safeties, schools they had to attend because they'd gotten wait-listed or sent in their deposits too late, schools their parents picked because they'd offered more scholarship money, because they were closer to home. My task is one of discernment. Less than two percent will make it in and it is my job to winnow them from the other ninety-eight percent, the chaff.

Roger knows this, so when I do not answer, he puts down the paper and looks at me guiltily, saying, "It's okay if you're busy. You don't have to come."

It is a trick. Roger is a ventriloquist with the truth. Though his mouth says, "You don't have to," his eyes say, *Please, please, please.*

He closes the passenger door behind me, walks around to his side. "I know I should have done this sooner," he says. "I just feel it needs a woman's touch. I won't know what's what. Maybe we'll even find some things we can use. It'll be whatever you say. If you say something goes, it goes. If you say it stays—"

"—I get it." I turn on the car radio, not caring what I hear. Just so long as it is loud. Just so long as I don't have to listen to him. I do not have to be polite. It is enough that I have agreed to come.

As we put New Jersey behind us, Roger sits stiffly, shoulders rigid as he drives, occasionally glancing my way. He wants me to turn down the volume, but he will not dare ask. His favors are all used up. We know each other well.

Roger's mother lived her adult life in a rent-controlled two-bedroom apartment in Brownsville on a street of identical housing projects. Side by side, their uniform blondish brick faces, bone white concrete stoops, and metal green doors announce the poverty of its inhabitants. His mother lived in the corner building and all of the stoops except hers are littered with people out for the day, which feels like summer come early. Young mothers sit on the lowest steps, idly pushing babies in strollers. Boys sit higher up or lean on the railings, playing music. We park in front of a stoop two doors down from his mother's place. A girl sits on the top step, a boy two steps below her. He sits between her knees, arms hooked over her thighs. The people on these stoops knew Roger's mother and they all called her Miss Mac (Roger's last name is MacGooden). In the four years I knew her, I never bothered to call her anything.

I take the key from him and enter first. Roger carries a handful of heavy-duty trash bags inside; they billow behind him, ghost-like, specters of things long past. Roger's mother was a smoker (though this is not what killed her) and the apartment is thick with the stale odor of smoke. I try not to breathe as I walk through the small square room to open the living room windows to air out the place. I'll start with the most difficult room first, just to set the tone. Heading to the master bedroom, I say, "Let's not linger."

His mother's bedroom closet is crammed with decades of rarely worn clothing. It takes but a glance to see that everything must go. As we bag his mother's clothing, Roger touches each item in passing, making everything take longer. With the exception of our wedding day where she'd dressed for the occasion, I'd seen his mother mostly in caftans and muu-muus, long or loose-fitting dresses that swallowed her shape. Her closet yields articles of clothing that come as a surprise. Trapeze tops, polyester pants and dresses with Peter Pan collars, bell sleeves and belted waists, reminiscent of things worn in *The Sound of Music*, crumble on brown wire hangers beneath the dry cleaner's original plastic.

Roger holds the black garbage bag, his face pained as he watches me pile everything in, but he does not protest. He has given me carte blanche and it is too late to take it back, but I can see how much the silence costs him. His eyes glassy with tears, his knuckles swollen from where the blood has rushed—he grips the garbage bag as though it is a lifeline—he holds the bag and lets me drop his mother's things in. If it were left up to him, he'd never be able to decide what to discard and what to keep. He'd try to find a way to bring it all home with us, although he knows we don't have the space. This is, after all, why he has brought me along. I am good at sorting things out, expert at making the tough calls.

Though it is a job for the work-study students in the admissions office, I am the one they send for when prospectives call in after the deadline has passed and they haven't yet heard from us. Impatient and hopeful, they call on the chance that their acceptances have been lost in the mail or that we have somehow simply forgotten to notify them to join the incoming class. If I am not busy, I'm the one the office staff gets to tell them we have denied their admission and their official letter is forthcoming. The work-study students are too afraid to hurt someone's feelings. They make it too personal and end up making things worse. The trick to delivering bad news is to be swift about it, so that the surprise tempers the pain. When they call me to the phone, I know it is not personal, though there is a person on the other end. I look at the prospective's name on the file on the screen before me, knowing I will never use it. I do not get overly familiar. I begin with "I regret to inform you," and, after reading our form denial letter to them, I pause—deliberately—to give them time to make sense of what I have said. On the other end, they are pausing too, to see if there is more, to see if there has been a mistake, to see if I will take it back, to see if we have enough space to squeeze in one additional student. When it is clear that there is nothing else, they thank me and hang up. I always let them hang up first. It is better that way; it gives the callers a sense of empowerment, makes them feel as if they are the ones doing the rejecting, after all. Sometimes, after the brief pause, they do not say thank you. Instead, they slam down the phone. Sometimes, they hang up before I even finish, but I never make it personal. I am good at what I do.

The bag of clothing nearly full, I feel Roger's eyes on me. "What?"

"Nothing," he says, continuing to look. He points to a bundled dress on the top of the pile, visible between the plastic. As I gather the opposite edges of the garbage bag to twist them into a knot, Roger darts his hand into the bag and caresses a green polyester dress. "She wore this to my middle school graduation."

This is the first time Roger has been to his mother's apartment since selecting the outfit she was buried in. He knew as well as I that the apartment needed to be cleaned out, but couldn't bring himself to do it and I hadn't had the heart to force him. I had never been on friendly terms with his mother and now that she was gone, I felt a measure of remorse for the distance kept between us.

It began at our wedding reception, with her coming over to the raised table where Roger and I sat with the bridal party. His mother raised a flute of sparkling cider and toasted us, saying, "Now you're part of the family."

Surely, she had meant to be welcoming, but I was young—just twenty-two—and it had seemed to me that she had just then sucked all of the air from our lives. I had understood my wedding vows literally, viewing Roger and I as brand new people, believing we were now each other's family. I had envisioned the two of us starting out together on an uncharted path and—before my eyes—that path had become sullied, trampled by the indifferent and muddied footprints of another.

When we are finally done with the closet, I send Roger to the kitchen to wrap and box the good china, the only thing I've identified as worth keeping. In the living room, I stoop to pick up unfinished knitting projects—half-finished sweaters, woolly mittens and frilly shawls in faded colors—from the floor around the armchair. Once the bag is full, I tie a wide, loose knot in its neck and call for Roger. "Can you throw this out?"

Though full, the bag is remarkably light. Roger holds it aloft, easily. "What's in here?"

"Just some knitting," I say. "Can you bring up the rest of the boxes from the car?"

After he has gone, I return to his mother's bedroom with two garbage bags to dump out the dresser drawers.

The scarred cherrywood bureau is cluttered with framed pictures, a bible, an address book, a piggy bank and empty packets of Alka-Seltzer. Most of the pictures are of Roger before I ever knew him. I pick up each one and search for his face beneath the layers of dust. It is easy to see that he is altogether a different man now.

The top left drawer is filled with bloomers, the right with odds and ends. Roger's mother never threw anything away. Scissors, a small sewing kit, a pack of sewing needles, pennies, dried out pens, black bobby pins, expired coupons, yellowed handkerchiefs, nylon balls of knotted knee-his, and a black lacquered jewelry box. I open the lid and music tinkles faintly in the stale air. The velvet bed of the box holds worthless costume jewelry, strands of fake pearls with their surfaces rubbed away to reveal the glass underneath. These are not my mother's things; they do not move me.

I open the bedroom windows to let in some fresh air. On the stoop below, Roger stands with the black garbage bag in his hand, clenching its neck, strangling the bag indifferently. His face tilted upwards, his stance is fixed, as if looking at something in the distance. There are only four steps separating him from the end of the stoop, yet he does not dump the garbage. Between the stoops, squat concrete sheds with blue metal doors provide a discreet method of disposal, preventing residents from having to line their curbs with unsightly trash. Roger had played atop these sheds as a young boy. He'd shown me the way the boys would get a running start and leap up onto the sheds, the smaller boys having to hoist. The sheds could be home in a game of Tag, or a base in a game of stickball, anything a poor boy could imagine. If he would only walk down the remaining four steps, he'd be able to go to those sheds and dump the bag he clutches with such a death grip and be done with it for once and for all.

Two stoops down from Roger, the girl takes a wide-toothed comb and parts her boyfriend's thick, unruly hair. Turning his head to the side, she combs out a section just along his ear and begins to braid his hair in cornrows. Nimbly, she braids his hair, evoking order out of chaos.

The metal railing burns beneath my hand. I stop midway down the stoop and come to Roger's side. "Doing okay?"

Roger continues to stare, but when I look toward the sun to see what he sees, I don't see anything.

"I can't do it," he says. His hand shakes from holding the neck of the bag so tightly. Roger leans against me, his coarse hair scratching through the thin fabric of my blouse, his face turned from me as he cries softly—politely—so as not to disturb.

"Want some help?" I ask, at a loss. There is no script for this moment between us.

Roger looks up, eyes me warily, as if this is some kind of a trick. We both know this is not something I can do for him. We both know I have done all I can. He shakes his head against me. "No," he says. Then softly, "Thanks."

I cup his shoulder, rub my hand lightly up and down his arm. The bag falls open and it is hard to know whether Roger has given up and let it go, or it if has merely slipped his grasp. Unfinished sweaters, shawls, and mittens spill onto the sidewalk like brightly colored innards, unraveling as they fall.

We do not pick them up.

If I listen closely, I can hear the rejected applicants when they cry. During that pause, while they are waiting for me to undo what I have done, I can hear them pull themselves together. When they thank me before hanging up, their voices—tremulous and confused—give it away. They clear their throats, struggling to make themselves seem un-affected, but if you listen, you can hear how hard it is to let go.

WHAT MATTERS MOST

YOU ARE on the way to your tango lesson with Tavares, the new young Puerto Rican teacher the center has hired to teach half of the Latin dance classes while Esmerelda takes a leave to have her baby. You are in the bathroom squinting under the bright lights, trying to see if the anti-aging anti-wrinkle serum you applied is working any miracles for you. It is not. Fine lines feather the frail brown skin near the sides of your eyes when you squint before you realize that squinting defeats the purpose of buying age-resistant makeup. You are applying lipstick when the phone rings.

It's your ex-husband. He doesn't even say hello when you pick up. "I would like to be there. It's only fair since you had her all Thanksgiving," he says.

Remind him that not only did he have her for Labor Day and Columbus Day, but that the two of you are splitting your daughter for the Christmas holidays. Warn him not to get greedy.

"You can't block me out, Viv. I'm still a part of your life, you know. As long as we have Brooke, I always will be. Like it or not," he says.

"Not," you say and hang up before he can get bring up his favorite topic and start asking for reconciliation. Remind yourself that getting rid of your husband was a good thing. Blot your lipstick and head out the door to go to your tango lesson.

Walk to the cross. At that moment in Argentine Tango between the fifth and sixth step, with all your weight balanced on your left foot, lean in closer and forget about all of the things that really matter. Forget to worry about Brooke coming home for mid-winter recess, forget that Tavares is your teacher and not your lover, forget that you are in your forties and he is not.

Tavares frowns at your sloppy dancing and tightens his hold on your arm, "Wiggle arms! Be firm! Brace your arm against mine. This is not salsa!"

"I can't help it." Whine as he pulls you from the cross into forward ochos. Love the ochos, feel the turns, the back and forth. You know the two of you look fantastic on the dance floor.

"You're never going to learn. You never pay attention."

"But I *am!*" Snap out of your reverie in time to see him shake his head at you in that annoying way of his. *Old woman*, you know he is thinking.

"You would still be better off taking the group class. That way you could switch partners with each song and—"

Cut him off. Lower your voice until you are purring. Tell him you can only learn with him. "Lead me into the forward ochos again and I'll show you." Touch his arm lightly.

One. Two. Three. Four. "Don't just dance like wood!" He half drags you once again to the cross.

"Don't yell!"

"Don't pout," he says as he pulls you into forward ochos. Close your eyes when you feel him signal a gancho; try not to take that extra half step like you always do. Come chest to chest with Tavares again before he can lead the tango close. Stand on your tiptoes and press into him before you open your eyes. "See?"

"*Vivian.*"

"Okay, okay. Once more?"

Tavares releases you and looks at his watch. Take a look too, trying not to stare at the way the thick dark hairs on his arm almost curl over the watch face. You know that there are moments between the two of you when he doesn't see your checkbook or your age. Like when he walks you to the cross and spins you out into ochos and lets his hand press against your back with more firmness than is necessary. There have been more moments like that than you can count. But you want to tell Brooke about him first, before you let this thing become. Wonder how Brooke would feel about Tavares being young and Puerto Rican. You raised your daughter with an open mind, tried to instill values in her that sank deeper and wider than mere culture, but Brooke has turned out to be an insufferable snob despite your efforts. And you're not just saying that because you're her mother. Brooke's last three crushes have all been on boys from Third World countries. Their suffering is what attracts her. Doubt that Brooke would think Tavares has suffered enough.

"Pay attention!" he says, as you step back on the wrong foot. Suppress the urge to tell him that you love him and that at night sometimes you can't sleep because there is this thing inside you that you can't explain. A feeling like heaviness, like a lot of weight slowly crushing you. When that happens all of the words go out of your head and you feel like you are suffocating.

"Get your head out of the clouds. Your time is up."

"Oh. Right."

He smiles at you. "You have remembered that the session ends next week, right?"

Actually, you forgot. "Next week? Already?" Tavares fills up your Thursday evenings from 6:30 to 7:50. Realize that you have no idea what to do with a free Thursday.

He walks to the far end of the studio to turn the music off and locks the cabinet that holds the stereo.

"Then it picks up the week after, right?"

"No. We have a month off for Intercession."

"Then you teach again?"

"I don't do session two. Esme does. She had a girl. She'll be back in time to take over again."

Esmerelda has legs no middle-aged woman should have. They put Tina Turner's to shame. Only her face shows her real age. The sun took its toll on her. Deep lines of age wrinkle her upper lip and crow's feet pull at the sides of her weathered brown face, making it look as if someone were standing behind her and gripping her hair hard from the back. It's a face you don't like to look at. You are glad she is on leave. She is having her baby at forty-six. You would never have a baby that late in life.

Remind Tavares that your daughter will be home next Friday. Ask if he's still having dinner with the two of you when she gets in.

Tavares looks up from changing his shoes. "How could I forget about the wonderful Brooke? She's all you talk about, all you think about."

Say, "That's not true." Use your most coquettish voice. Let it imply that you think of other things, such as him.

Tavares looks up at you. His eyes linger longer than necessary.

This is one of those moments.

Sometimes having coffee with a good friend is the best thing you can do and all you can hope for. Especially after five new messages from your ex-husband with suggestions about the ways you, he and Brooke could enjoy her mid-winter recess as a family. You are sitting on a stool at the island in the middle of your kitchen the next morning, surrounded by hardwood floors that gleam from a fresh waxing, twirling around in circles on the stool as if you are a teenager from the fifties hanging out at the local diner. No matter that your coffee stands cold and untouched on the counter or that the good friend you are imagining is none other than your housekeeper, Abby. Abby is in the kitchen pulling lettuce apart for a salad and you have not even offered her any coffee.

Abby is in her mid-to-late forties, just slightly older than you, but Abby seems much older. Watch Abby and understand that although you are both black and near in age that the similarities end there. Tick off a list of points in your mind to remind you of just how dissimilar the two of you are:

1. Abby acts old, walking around in senior citizen clothing fresh from a rack at K-Mart, while you make sure to feel and look and act young. You watch your weight. You keep abreast of all the latest trends. You have a personal trainer. You still wear your blue jeans tight.

2. Abby is a widow and not a divorcee like yourself. Therefore, Abby is prone to lapse into long droning family stories about her dead Nelson and her children. Abby whips out photos of grand babies at the drop of a hat. You, being divorced, are close-mouthed on the subject of your ex-husband. He is the last thing you want to talk about.

3. Abby has only finished high school. She's never gone to college unlike you who have both your undergraduate and graduate degrees from prestigious institutions.

4. Abby is forgetful when it comes to her children. She has so many of them—three boys and two girls—that she can afford to mix up their birthdays and call one by the other's name. You have the one daughter, Brooke, so you have to be very very careful of her.

Rise and begin to dance the eight basic steps of tango to imaginary music, making sure to extend your legs back far with each step. Pluck a daisy from the vase at the center of the kitchen's island and hold the stem between your teeth. Close your eyes and pretend that your left arm is around Tavares' neck.

"That's what you do every week in that class, Miss Vivian? Isn't that the kind with all the fancy stuff, where they drag you all over floor?" Abby asks.

Tell her, "No one drags me. We haven't gotten up to arrastres yet." The look on Abby's face is discomforting. She seems to be watching you in a way that says she is trying hard to no avail to imagine someone your age dancing like that. Feel Abby's gaze linger at the pinch of skin under your neck. Tilt your head down. Thwart her gaze. Feel Abby looking around your mouth for lines. Relax the muscles around your mouth accordingly and clench your jaw to tighten the skin under it. Remind yourself that you are not old. Remind yourself that Abby is a hag. And where does she get off pointing fingers anyway? Abby was old when you first hired her and she is even older now.

"You keep flowers in your mouth in class?" she asks.

"No. We don't have to. Tavares doesn't make us."

Abby's eyes light up with knowing and she puts the lettuce down. "Oh. *He's* teaching it?"

"That's not why I'm taking it!" you blurt before you can stop yourself.

"Of course not," Abby says. "I wasn't even thinking that."

"Tango is demure. It's got sophistication and class. It's all about grace and elegance. It's intricate, not like that salsa stuff Esme teaches which is just a bunch of wiggling."

Abby nods and changes the subject. "I have to get used to cooking for more than one person with Miss Brooke coming for vacation. You eat like a bird so it's not hard to get things ready for you—"

"Brooke definitely has an appetite," you cut in, happier to be talking about something else.

"Sure does. Last time she was here she ate like it was the Last Supper!"

"She's a starving student. You know what they say about cafeteria food." You smile with thoughts of your own boarding school days. You reach out and lay your hand on Abby's, momentarily forgetting about your differences.

Abby flinches and stares at your fingers draped lightly over her own. Look at your fingers. See them not as though they are the fingers you have lived with all your life, but as if they do not belong to you. See them as Abby might see them. Long brown fingers still smelling of scented lotion with weekly manicured nails shaped in tapering ovals. Fingers that have never had to become wrinkled while wringing a mop in its bucket. Or remain in a sink full of grimy dishwater. Or curl around the handle of an iron. Or tuck in the elastic of a fitted sheet. Lazy fingers. Idle and rich. You've never seen them this way before. Wiggle them to shake off the shame. Remind yourself that Abby could have had the same things you had if she'd wanted. No one ever hand-ed you anything on a silver platter.

"That's right," Abby says as if there's been no break in the conver-sation, "And Miss Brooke sure has a lot of favorite foods. Guess I better go to the market and pick up some things so I can start getting them ready for her." She delicately pulls her hand out from under yours and heads for the door, leaving you with the distinct feeling of being dismissed.

Once Abby leaves, you run a bath and soak in it. Allow your mind to wander, even though it always comes back to Brooke. Wonder if Brooke will ever forgive you for sending her away and if you can ever know if Brooke has forgiven you. Realize that you don't know your daughter anymore. Sixteen years old and already Brooke is a stranger to you. She had come back after the first trimester of boarding school a changed woman. You had not recognized her. She'd cut off her shoul-der length hair—the hair that you had diligently oiled and braided and brushed and helped her grow and take care of for years—to get rid of the perm. She'd worn short baby dread locks that reminded you of a pickaninny's pigtails you'd seen on Civil War memorabilia in the mu-seums. The next vacation had brought even more changes. After last year's mid-winter break, Brooke decided to become a vegetarian and join an animal rights group. She came home in the dead of a snowy New York winter wearing canvas sneakers and a cotton jacket because she decided that since she no longer ate animals she shouldn't wear them either. You put up with these changes because it is the only way to keep her and because you sense that these rebellions are directed at yourself. You accept the blame because you and your ex-husband agreed that it wouldn't be fair for only one of you to keep Brooke while you hammered out the terms of your divorce and the custody terms and that it would prevent one parent from unfairly hogging her if you sent her to Lyman-Sankey, a boarding school in western Massachusetts, and split the costs. So you bought your daughter herbal shampoos and conditioners with jojoba to encourage hair growth and you had Abby stock up on soy milk, soybean butter, tofu, tempeh and textured vegetable protein.

Next week, you are fifteen minutes late for your last session with Tavares. He lights into you about being late and irresponsible and wasting his time and your money and not bothering to call or reschedule —right in front of Esmerelda who is there showing off her baby to a couple practicing a milonga basic in front of the mirrored wall. The couple discreetly leaves the practice room, but Esme takes her time and throws a look at you that is vengeful and satisfied. In the middle of Tavares' tirade, you take comfort in the fact that Esme's legs are getting older and it will take her more than a few weeks to work off the fat she gained from her baby.

Tell Tavares that you are not a child and that he can't yell at you that way. Slowly remove your jacket, fold it and lay it on the window ledge. Change into the dance shoes that make you two inches taller and put your street shoes in a corner by the radiator.

"Well, you act like one," Tavares says as he walks away from you and opens the cabinet that contains the stereo.

"Go to hell, Tavares. Where do you get off yelling at me like that in front of everybody?"

He turns the volume up high and the music takes over the room, filling it so that it feels like the orchestra is right there in the room with you.

"Tango position!" he commands as he jerks your right hand into position and braces his forearm against yours. "In front of everybody?" Tavares mocks you, his voice a strained falsetto in imitation of you. "You see?" he says, roughly pulling you to him. "It's so damn important to you to look good in front of everybody."

"That's not true!"

"It is. You're just a big baby." His fingers dig into your back.

"You're hurting me!"

"So set on having everything your way!"

"Fuck you!"

"You you you. The world does not revolve around you, Vivian! You think you're the only one that matters, the only one that's important, right?" The look on his face is terrible. His voice drops to a whisper. "And it's more important for you to show Esme up than for you to have the common courtesy to tell me you're sorry for standing me up and being late."

"And what the hell are you? Bitching and moaning like some prima donna! I was just a little late. I couldn't help it. Brooke is coming and everything has to be perfect! I have to get everything right. You just don't understand."

You don't mean to cry, but you can't seem to help it, what with the music so loud in your ears that you can hardly think and Tavares so mad at you and dancing you so fast you can barely keep up without tripping and holding you so close and rough that you almost can't breathe and your daughter coming and you being scared everything will go wrong. You cry right there in the middle of the scuffed floor with the radiator behind you and the mirrored wall before you and Tavares and the music and Brooke and all the things that matter caving in on you all at once. "I'm sorry!" you scream and pull out of his grasp.

Then Tavares' hands are wiping your tears and you think he is apologizing because he'd forgotten about Brooke, but the condoleons and violins and all the other string instruments whose names you have never learned are so loud that you can't hear well enough to be sure since he is whispering again. Then he is kissing you, kissing you and walking you to the cabinet and lifting you on top of it, fumbling with the latch on his belt, running his hands up your legs, pushing roughly at the hem of your skirt—you feel the softness of his hands, hands without calluses, and know without a doubt that Brooke would not think he has suffered enough.

Pull into the parking lot at Lincoln Center the next day. For some reason, the administrators at your daughter's school have chosen Lincoln Center as the drop-off place for the kids taking the chartered bus into New York. Kids Brooke's age mill about the three large buses, saying their good-byes and waiting for their rides to come get them. They all have a look about them that you can't place. If you did not know they came off the bus together, you would still know that they were a group. They slouch and tilt and lean forward when they talk to one another, standing like they are too cool to stand straight. You can't tell the boys from the girls. They are all dressed in baggy jeans, ski caps and big bulky down coats. Except for Brooke, who you can pick out right away. She is the only one not dressed for the weather. A thin denim jacket covers her bony shoulders and arms and you don't have to guess that she didn't bother to wear her thermals like you reminded her to. The navy blue paisley swirls of her bandanna cover her growing dreadlocks; the bottom half of her cherubic brown face is hidden by the upturned collar of her denim jacket. You can't see her nose, but you know that it is running. You grab the raincoat you keep in the backseat and get out of the car, eager to cover up your poor freezing daughter. An Asian girl with a waif thin body and bright orange hair passes her a cigarette, but when she sees you, she refuses the smoke.

"Hey Mom," Brooke says as you hand her a tissue and motion for her to blow her nose. She allows you to hug her for the briefest of seconds. You feel her thin fingers push at the tops of your arms when you have hugged long enough.

"You must be freezing to death out here with nothing on!"

"No, it's cool," she says. "This is Ji-In Kim."

"Hello Ji-In. Here Brooke, this will keep you warmer. Put this on."
You try to help her into the raincoat, but she backs away and looks at
you as if you are asking her to eat arsenic.

"What's that made out of?"

"It's perfectly safe. Plastic. Vinyl. No animals."

She takes the raincoat from you and eyes it warily. After Ji-In puts
out her cigarette, she eyes it, too. Brooke turns it inside out and thumps
the lining. "What about this?"

"It's padded."

"With what? Down? Feathers?"

She's got you there. "I don't know," you say.

"I'm not putting that on. No way."

Ji-In nods and agrees with Brooke, even though she is wearing a
pair of calf-high leather boots.

"Okay fine, Brooke. Then let's just get you in the car. Where's
your stuff?"

"Dad's getting it."

"What?" Breathe slowly. Maybe you have misheard.

She shrugs and gives you her *don't weird out on me* look. "Dad showed
up a little bit before you. I thought you guys had worked something out
or something. You're not going to do anything are you?"

"Like what, Brooke? What would I do?"

"I don't know, Mom. Just please, okay? Just be cool."

Tell her that you're the coolest and watch her roll her eyes again.
You are losing points quickly.

As if he knows he is being talked about, your ex-husband comes up
to you. He is carrying one of Brooke's duffel bags in each hand as if
they are lightweight. They are not. You've seen her pack before. Your
ex-husband has grown a paunch. He doesn't look so hot since your divorce, but you know you have never looked better. Feel a slight twinge
of satisfaction when you notice that he knows this too.

"What are you doing here?"

"You were late."

"Five minutes! Give me a break. Besides, it takes you more than five minutes to get here. So what were you doing? Spying on me?" From the corner of your eye, you see Brooke frown and whisper with Ji-In. You hear her say, "My parents are like so immature."

"No, Viv, I was not spying on you." Then he smiles and looks at you like you are crazy. "Don't be so dramatic."

"Dramatic?" you shriek as Brooke tries to blend in with the background behind you, too ashamed to acknowledge her relationship to you. "You have a lot of nerve. I don't know how you can dare to show up here. This is a violation of the court agreement," you say, wishing you had your can of pepper spray with you.

You snatch Brooke by the arm roughly and pull her over to you as if there is a white line etched in the ground between you and your ex-husband. If you gave her the chance to choose sides, you might lose. But for now—for this weekend at least—you can choose for her.

"*I* have Brooke for the recess. *You* don't."

He shrugs boyishly. "Well, I told you I wanted to see her. And I didn't have any other plans for the weekend. And I figured if you could see that I was serious about spending time with the two of you, then maybe you would come around. Come on, Viv."

You are so angry that you can't speak for a good minute. You can't believe him and his nerve and you don't appreciate the way he is acting all innocent and making you look like the bad guy who won't play fair.

Maybe you'd come around.

You remember that shrug and that phrase from countless times in your marriage when he coerced you into doing something you had already said you didn't want to do. Like when he took the job in New York without telling you until it was a done deal, even though you said you didn't want to leave Philadelphia. He took it and hoped that maybe you'd come around to the idea of living in the Big Apple. Like the nights when you wanted to be left alone and he put his hand on your thigh or breast and continued, because he wanted you and was hoping that maybe you'd come around. And when you told him to stop, he kept on going, hoping, just hoping that maybe you'd come around.

You could kill him right now with your bare hands for his assuming you'd come around.

Say, "I don't think so," and take the duffel bags away from him, even though they weigh more than you do and your arms feel like they are popping out of their sockets.

"You don't have to be like this, Viv," he says. "What about dinner at least?"

"I'm already having someone else over for dinner that I want Brooke to meet," you say. Shoulder the bags and walk away.

"So you're the famous Brooke! Or should I say infamous?" Tavares says when you let him in. He kisses your cheek briefly and then engulfs Brooke in a bear hug after giving her a small bouquet he'd picked up for her. The arrangement is cheap—yellow, white, and pink daisies, carnations, and baby's breath—with not a single zinnia or gladiola in sight. You think it's a bit overdone, but Brooke loves it. She blushes under the attention and basks in it. It makes her happy and more at ease and that is all that matters.

Tavares and his cheap flowers have made more leeway with your daughter in less than five minutes than you have all afternoon. Your initial greeting had been strained. Brooke rebuffed your attempts to hug and kiss her. She didn't appreciate your efforts to keep her room exactly the way she'd left it the last time. She hugged Abby and thanked her for preparing her favorite pasta dish, a dish Abby could not have made had you not paid for the groceries.

You feel like an outsider. Throughout the morning and afternoon— with Abby and Brooke watching *Oprah* and *Jennie Jones* and *Ricki Lake* while Abby intermittently cooked and gossiped and now through a dinner peppered with questions directed to Tavares about the living conditions in Puerto Rico and the poverty in parts of the island that didn't attract tourism and the depletion of its natural resources as a result of that tourism and the history of Argentine Tango and Tavares' initial interest in studying it and the two years he spent in Argentina and whether or not tango really had African origins and the differences between Argentine Tango and Ballroom or American Style Tango— you feel as if you are on the outside looking in. And the feeling sickens you. Briefly, over salad and during the beginning of the meal, wonder if that sick feeling in your stomach is pregnancy and for five hysterical moments your mind is filled with anxiety over the possibilities of getting pregnant so soon as a result of last night with Tavares and having a change of life baby at your age like Esmerelda which is too reprehensible to bear. You look across the table at Tavares. He is wearing an olive green shirt with the first two buttons left open so that you can see a vee of golden brown flesh and chest hair. His sleeves are rolled up to his elbows. Dark curling hairs circle and hide the dusky skin of his forearms. His hands, large and brown, drum idly on the white linen tablecloth and he leans back in his chair, eyeing you with sureness. Don't let him distract you. Try to forget how handsome he is. That is what got you into trouble in the first place. Run off a list of points on how you feel about the possibility of having his baby:

1. He is too young. Fatherhood would be a joke to him until he matured.

2. He is Puerto Rican. He will teach the baby Spanish and you won't be able to understand your own child.

3. He has no money and will probably fight you for custody. He might even make you pay him child support.

4. Having his baby might cast a shadow on your character and destroy your chances of winning custody of Brooke. The judge might think you easy and desperate, fast and loose, unfit to raise a precocious teenager and set a good example.

You come to your senses once the pasta is served, deciding that you are merely nervous and not pregnant. After pasta and dessert, usher the two of them into the den to show off some pictures of your daughter.

Tavares comments on an eighth grade photo of Brooke winning a debate, "Early on your daughter was showing the signs of becoming a very beautiful girl."

"Thank you," you and Brooke say at the same time.

When you go to the dining room to clear the table, Tavares follows you.

"What's wrong?" he asks, kissing your neck. "You look really tired."

"She hates me!"

"No. She's a bit high strung like her mother. She's got a lot of pride like her mother. And she thinks that she's got a lot to prove—"

"Like her mother," you and Tavares say at the same time.

"You have a knack for that," he teases you.

"Do you think she likes me?"

"I don't think this is as big of a deal to her as it is to you. I think you should relax and calm down and let whatever happens happens. That's what I do," he says. You can't help wondering if that was how he explained last night to himself. "After all, she's here now. You have the whole weekend to win her over. It doesn't have to be done in one night. She's here. With you. Let that be all that matters for the moment."

Tell him he's right. "What about you? Do you like her? Because she sure seems taken with you. 'Tavares, was there ever a time in Puerto Rico when you didn't have hot water to bathe in? Tavares, did you ever have to wear hand-me-downs? Is it very hard to learn the tango, Tavares? How do you feel about factory farming, or wearing wool, Tavares?'"

"Don't make fun," he says. "It's good to hold a pretty girl's interest and have her look at you like you're ten feet tall. If she were a few years older—"

"Then it wouldn't be illegal."

"In my country, a girl like her would already be married."

"This *is* your country."

"Some things we do different. My mother married when she was fourteen. She had me when she was Brooke's age. In Puerto Rico, your daughter would be a woman."

Say, "That's enough, Tavares. I can bring the rest of these dishes into the kitchen myself." The joking had been funny at first. You don't mind being ribbed a bit, but some jokes can go too far.

Go into the dining room for the last plate. Brooke follows you back into the kitchen. Make a mental note to take her clothes shopping while she's here and insist that she buy some decent clothing. She is wearing a tight orange ballerina top that hints at breasts she'll never have. Her tiny waist is belted tightly; bright blue baggy jeans with a big X on each pocket balloon over her small hips and down her legs and are cuffed over the tops of faded canvas sneakers that have been patched with duct tape.

"So, is that your boyfriend or what?" she asks, plucking a spinach rotini from the plate in your hand and eating it.

In shock, you drop the plate you've been carrying to the garbage disposal. It clatters and crashes on your newly waxed floor, spreading tri-colored pasta all over the shine.

"Sorry Mom. I was just wondering that's all. I mean 'cause he's young and stuff and a lot of people's moms go through stuff like this when they get to be your age, but that's not cool. I mean, really, he's hot and everything, but he's not much older than me, you know?"

Lie.

Say, "He's just my teacher. That's all."

"That's cool, then. It just wouldn't make sense, that's all. Like, it would make more sense if I went out with him. Or somebody that's like my age, you know? Do you want me to help you clean that up? I know Abby won't be back till tomorrow and my work assignment is in the cafeteria, so I do this all the time."

"No, that's all right. Why don't you just go back to the den? I'll just be a few minutes cleaning up this mess. Ask Tavares to teach you to tango. Or show him your awards and soccer medals."

"Mom, it's no big deal."

Refuse her help. Hold onto the counter. "Just go sweetheart. Don't worry about this."

"You sure?"

"Yes. Sure. Go."

You don't feel the coldness of the floor as you get down on your hands and knees with a wet paper towel to pick up the jagged edges of plate that lie scattered across the floor. Tell yourself that it's not your fault that your daughter has become such a little bitch. Blame The Lyman-Sankey School, then remember that the decision to send her away was yours. It is your fault that you raised a daughter whom you love with a desperation bordering on insanity but with whom you cannot have a civil conversation. Wonder where Brooke learned to be so tactless and so shrewd. Oh yes, you understood the underlying threat. You heard it loud and clear. Laugh it off as absurd that you should compete with your daughter. You love Tavares, but you would give up a hundred Tavareses to be able to talk to Brooke without feeling sharp, needling pain.

Wonder if talking about Tavares could be the door-opener you need to make inroads with your daughter. You could tell Brooke how you feel about all of it. Brooke is a bright girl, a high school sophomore. She will listen and analyze. Then she will decide that you are having a mid-life crisis. You don't want her to think that. Mid-life crisis. For men it's buying a red sports car and chasing eighteen- year- old girls. For you, it's tango lessons and a twenty-something year old Puerto Rican. You don't want Brooke to see it that way. You feel the need to convince her otherwise choking you, overwhelming you. Spring from the floor to go tell your daughter the truth.

The den is empty although the green power light of the stereo is still on. You go to Brooke's room next. Stop in front of her door. You hear something. Push the door open slightly; a shaft of light triangles on your daughter's empty bed. You hear voices, soft and hushed, off the terrace. Follow the muffled voices until you see the silhouettes of their bodies through the balcony curtains. They are leaning over the railing, staring up at the skyline, talking and having fun without you. Brooke leans into Tavares' side and his strong brown fingers twist and stroke her dreadlocks. Try not to notice how youthful their bodies look together, like two willows bending towards each other. Brooke points up at something you can't see and Tavares laughs deep and long. Brooke joins in and pushes him lightly, just enough to tease. You step closer and strain to hear the joke. It would be good to laugh right now, but whatever they are saying is lost to you.

You know it's not the words that matter.

Press down on the balls of your feet. Feel your calves flex and tighten. Throw your head back and straighten your posture like Tavares taught you. Then remember that you have already had your last lesson.

A CUP OF MY TIME

THE TWO BOYS are fighting inside of me. I can feel them doing it, making a commotion, sapping all of my energy. I make it to the bathroom and slap a wet washcloth over my forehead, dragging it down over my eyes and cheeks as I try to do deep breathing. Now I see hollows and shadows in my face where before I only saw beauty. I am worn. Dead skin collects on my face because I have no time to slough it off. Dark circles grow under my eyes in widening rings. It is the fault of these babies, these twins, these embryos, these fetuses—I really do not care what you call them—moving inside of me. According to our doctor, these babies are battling it out inside of my womb ("like Jacob and Esau inside of Rebekah," she said, as if that reference had any meaning for me). Sharing the same placenta, they are fighting within my body, each one trying to appropriate a larger portion of blood and nutrients for himself. Cary doesn't know it, but I have named our fighting twins: Sanjay and Sanjiv. Sanjiv, the larger boy getting most of the blood, is at risk of heart failure, while the smaller Sanjay is starving. Today the pain is worse, making me imagine tiny little fists concealing knives, brass knuckles and nun chucks. I imagine sucker punches and black eyes and all out brawls. These twins are duking it out inside of me, kicking my ass.

Once I return to the living room, I hear Mrs. Majumdar outside on the stoop. I can hear her all the way up here on the second floor.

Her voice isn't so much loud as it is thick. It presses all the air out of this living room and surrounds me, closing in like walls. I reach behind me for the arm of the nearest chair and lower myself into it, listening to Mrs. Majumdar as she scolds her husband's cousins. I'd seen the two earlier when I'd staggered up those stairs. They'd been sitting in the same spot all day long, nesting like pigeons. For the past week, they'd been living above me on the third floor of the triplex. "Pradeep! Rohit! You know better than to be lounging around like lazy lazy boys. You're bringing down the value of my property. Tomorrow you go to your uncle's restaurant. We'll put you boys to work. Now upstairs with you."

Mrs. Majumdar's English is followed by a scolding in Punjabi, which I do not understand. My grandparents put it away like so much old luggage when they left Amritsar after the Partition. They never handed it down to my parents who never handed it down to me.

The pain subsides as Mrs. Majumdar talks. Her voice calms the twins inside of me, even though they are hearing it through a sac of viscous liquid, a mound of flesh, and a wall of plaster, sheetrock and brick.

I rise with difficulty, preparing to make my way to the front door.

Cary appears by my side and steadies my elbow. "Need some help?"

"Where did you come from?" Every morning Cary rises at six, the same as when he was going to campus to teach. Now, he locks himself in our other bedroom—the room meant for Sanjay and Sanjiv—which has become Cary's makeshift office, at least until the end of his sabbatical.

"Who can write anything with all of her racket?" he asks.

Living here was his idea. Now that he's on leave and so much underfoot, he notices how vocal Mrs. Majumdar is and how frequent are her visits. She comes upstairs every day to borrow something from me.

Mrs. Majumdar knocks on our door. My husband pleads, "Don't let her in Sona. Not today, all right?"

I am already waddling toward the door. "I have to," I say. "She's our landlord."

"For all the time she spends in our apartment, she should be paying us rent," he says. After the words come out, he smiles at me sideways, trying to pass it off as a joke. He disappears, cloistering himself, before I even reach the door.

I open the door and Mrs. Majumdar comes in, removing her chunni from her hair, letting it drop to her shoulders. "Sonali, did you see those boys? Those lazy urchins I have to call my kin?"

"I saw them earlier when I was outside."

She adjusts her glasses. "Eh? Outside? You should stay in here resting. If you need something and Cary is not around, Pradeep and Rohit will go for you. They don't have anything else to do."

"It sounds like you'll be putting them to work," I say.

"Eh? So you heard? Tomorrow they'll be sorry! Once my husband gets them, they'll never know what it means to be idle." Mrs. Majumdar takes a seat on the couch. Her pajama-like salwars bunch beneath her.

"That should be a good learning experience." They keep the lights low in Kaur and Singh so that you don't see how badly the place is in need of repairs. The ceiling there is made of popcorn stucco and the concrete stalactites hang over the patrons' heads, years and years out of code. "You've been nothing but kind to them."

"Who are you telling? Do you think they appreciate anything? Last night, I went upstairs to check the radiators, and I asked them 'Where else do you think you can get the whole third floor and pay nothing? Nowhere! I could have tenants in that unit and be bringing in some real money, but I give it to you lazy rascals who don't even appreciate. What do you give me? Nothing! You don't even cut the grass out front for me! Winter will come and you probably won't even shovel the snow.'"

"That's the least they could do." I set a cup of tea and a platter of biscuits in front of her.

"The very least! The money I could be making. That apartment could have been filled. They don't know how lucky they are to find it vacant. If they had been a week later? Well, who knows?" Mrs. Majumdar says. She pours milk into her tea, bites into the sweet crunchy cookie and brushes crumbs from her kameez.

It wouldn't have mattered if her husband's cousins had come a week or a month later, the upstairs apartment would have been vacant no matter what. Cary and I have been living here since he first began teaching, and the only person I'd ever known to live upstairs for any real length of time had been her daughter Geeta.

"I wonder, Sonali, if I could borrow a cup of sugar?" Mrs. Majumdar asks.

"Certainly."

On Monday it was sea salt. On Tuesday, it was milk. On Wednesday it was cumin. Today it is sugar, but I only have Splenda, sugar substitute. Not that it matters. Mrs. Majumdar has no interest in our meager staples. What she really wants is a cup of my time.

"Is Splenda all right?" I ask, measuring out the sugar substitute in the kitchen.

"Whatever you have will do nicely."

"Have you heard anything from Geeta?"

Mrs. Majumdar makes an exasperated sound, expelling wind past teeth. "That girl. Do you know how long it has been and I have heard nothing from her? I worry," she says. I barely remember her daughter Geeta. A tall willowy girl with a penchant for blue contact lenses, Jimi Hendrix and Eric Clapton, she'd loop "Purple Haze" or "Layla" and play the one song for three hours without stopping. Like her mother, she was more sound than woman to me, a blistering guitar blaring through my ceiling, bleeding down my walls.

As I search the kitchen cabinets, she recaps all of Geeta's major offenses, lost in her own world of self-pity. To tell the truth, I like Mrs. Majumdar's visits. They keep my mind occupied on someone else's pain. While Mrs. Majumdar complains and demands sympathy, I do not have to think about these babies tearing me apart. Listening to Mrs. Majumdar list Geeta's unjust treatment of her, I don't have to think about the weekly sonograms, or the possibility that without laser surgery to correct the unequal flow of blood, neither baby will survive. I do not have to think about my body and the world of conflict it carries.

With Mrs. Majumdar, I think only in terms of measurements. A half cup of milk, a pinch of sea salt, a tablespoon of cumin, a cup of sugar. These measurements block out the doctor's measurements, her pronouncements on my boys' meager lives, her words pouring out, "Sixty to seventy percent of the time both of the babies will die."

I pour the cupful into a baggie and zip it closed. When I reenter the living room, shaking the small pouch, Mrs. Majumdar is wiping her eyes with her chunni. She reaches up for the baggie, looks at me with red-rimmed eyes. "Soon you will know how it is. A mother always worries."

As soon as she leaves, Cary reemerges from his office. In honor of his sabbatical, he has ceased wearing shoes in the house. Walking around in stockinged feet, he slips into rooms without notice.

"Is she gone yet?" He touches my shoulder, then tries to wrap his arms around me from behind. After two unsuccessful attempts, he walks around to face me. He takes my hands in his, rubbing my palms with his thumbs.

"You know when she leaves down to the second," I say. "The incredible appearing man."

He buries his lips in my neck. "You smell like honey."

I touch his hair, letting my fingers sink into the thick sandy-colored strands. He's been growing his hair long since he's been on leave. Now his hair hangs over his eyes and curls at his ears and neck, thick and unruly. His hair turns up all around the house. I find it in the shower's drain and on our pillowcases. Just the other day, I found one of his hairs curled around a carton of milk in the refrigerator.

"When are you getting a haircut?"

"I hadn't thought about it."

"How about before the next doctor's visit? I want her to think we're a respectable couple."

"Having very respectable babies," he says. "Same time next week?"

I nod. Ever since they discovered my twins were sharing the same placenta, the doctor has been making us come in for weekly sonograms, but Cary always needs reminding.

"So, what did she want this time?"

"Sugar."

"She's got her own damned restaurant. Probably gets shipments of fifty pound bags of sugar and she wants sugar from us." He rubs the nape of my neck, and I lean into him. My stomach tightens and the upper portion of my abdomen fills with a sharp and debilitating pain that eclipses the earlier pain, making it seem merely unpleasant.

I latch onto Cary's arm, gripping it to keep myself upright and steady. "Call the doctor."

Used to the false alarms, Cary does not rush. Every time I have the slightest pain, we go to the hospital. Cary thinks I'm paranoid, but I remind him we have full coverage and excellent health insurance. Within their world inside of me, the boys have their own troubles, fighting for blood. They have their jobs, and I have mine. My fight is a battle of vigilance. Although the surgery that could save them is best done early into the pregnancy, each week the doctor says the boys are in too awkward of a position, that one false firing of the laser could tear their shared placenta and cause the twins to bleed to death. We can only wait and hope for them to move. Each time I feel anything, we come to the hospital.

"You did the right thing by coming in immediately. Your twins appear to have moved," the doctor says. Her voice conveys no emotion, as sterile as her gloved hands. "By tomorrow morning they should be in a favorable enough position for the procedure." She reminds me of the risks involved, tells me that I will only receive local anesthesia. I will have to be awake and still the entire time. She says that many things can go wrong while she attempts to cauterize the blood vessels. Once I am dressed again and about to leave, she says, "I have to prepare you. If the procedure fails to save the fetuses, the two of you will have a tough decision to make. You'll have to choose which one you want to live."

We have known the risks all along. We have known what we might have to do, but hearing it stated aloud in such a dispassionate manner, as if we are being asked to choose between DSL and dial-up, is more than we should have to bear. All the way home from the hospital I am crying. I start as soon as we climb into the cab and I am still crying when I climb into our bed.

Tomorrow, we will have to choose which child will have a chance at life. I think of my doctor's wan face and fantasize about hurting her. I feel power rush into my hands. It feels like I could twist the metal bars of our headboard into a pretzel if I wanted. "Either way, I guess she gets paid!" I cry. "How could she be so heartless?"

Cary defends her. "It was just a formality, Sona. She had to say it."

"How can she expect someone to choose? Why can't she save them both?"

"She'll try."

An emptiness spreads through me. No matter what Cary says to calm me, I cry and cry and cry. Cary tries to soothe me, but I will not let him. I am thinking of all that has been asked of me, all that I have given, all that I have eked out in order to help soothe others. I cry, wishing this cup would pass from me.

After some time, he gives up trying to console me. "Let's just try and get some sleep," he says. "Sona, do you want anything before we lie down? Can I bring you a cold compress or something?" he asks.

"No."

He climbs into the bed beside me. It is too early for sleep, but he turns off the lights and pulls the cover over us.

"You've got to try and take it easy, Sona," he says. "It will be all right."

"How? If we don't choose, both Sanjay and Sanjiv could die."

"They'll both survive," he says. Then, like an afterthought, "I like those names."

"What if they don't?" I ask. "What should we do then?"

Cary rubs my shoulders. "It's your body Sona. It should be your choice." He smiles, pleased with himself for saying what he believes to be the right thing.

I lock a word deep in my throat and my throat grows raw with holding it in. I wonder if my voice will now grow thick like Mrs. Majumdar's. If it will fill up this apartment and coat the walls like paint. If it will seep under the doors and sills and cracks and flow out onto the stoop and all the way to the curb until it has coated the street.

"I'm going to go turn out the lights in the living room. Do you want anything while I'm up?" Cary asks.

"No," I say. I do not care that he is trying to distract himself by being solicitous. I do not care that maybe this is tearing him apart too.

"Fine," he says, exasperated. Then, "Honey, are you sure? Isn't there anything I can do for you?"

How easily he can offer his support, knowing full well that his body won't be carrying a dead twin to term, knowing that when things get unpleasant he can always hide in his office and shut everything out, knowing that he is not a walking reminder of failure. "Pray?"

Cary sighs, smoothing my hair across the pillow. "I haven't prayed in a very long time. Not for anything. Not even that time when I thought you would leave," he says. "I don't know if I remember how."

"Fine," I say and Cary gets out of the bed.

"Fine," I say again even though there is no one to hear me, liking the sound of my own voice. The sound fills up my mouth. It fills up my lungs. It fills up my head. "Fine fine fine fine fine."

I can't hear him walk away from me, but I know he is in the living room double checking everything, making sure that we've locked the door, set the alarm, and that the lights won't burn through the evening and run our electric bill sky high. These are the things he can control. They give him a semblance of normalcy, allowing him to pretend that tonight is an ordinary night and we are an ordinary couple having ordinary babies. As long as he secures us for the night, he can pretend that—like so many other couples—the decisions we make are trivial, altering the lives of no one.

After some time, Cary returns and climbs back into bed beside me. "There's got to be something I can do for you," he says.

I say, "Yes."

"Tell me."

He scoots against me, curving his body into a spoon. His chin digs into my shoulder, his head rests heavy against the side of my face. I do not push him away. Lying beside him, I am preparing for tomorrow. I practice being still. "Sona?"

I say, "Choose."

INTERSECTIONS

JUST TO SEE HER, Jack waits in his car parked in front of a Kennedy Fried Chicken, a conspicuously inconspicuous white man in the Bedford-Stuyvesant section of Brooklyn, looking for all the world like an easy target. The Kennedy Fried Chicken has no Formica tables bolted to the floor and no chairs. Patrons are not meant to linger. Jack watches them crowd into the chicken joint, bustling in the small rectangle of space. They press against barriers of bulletproof plastic and have to shout their orders. They slide their money through and remove their two pieces, biscuits and sweet potato pies from a revolving cube. Directly outside, three boys loiter by a metal dumpster and pass a forty in a brown paper bag. Across the street, women clad in suits and shod in sneakers rise from the subway on Fulton and walk briskly, the straps of their shoulder bags slung across torsos instead of shoulders to deter snatchers. Gripped between index and middle fingers, innocuous house keys become weapons, ready to jab any offender in the eye, eager to maim. He cannot watch the women. Though he knows they are being smart, proactive even, about protecting themselves, it somehow seems to him that *they* are the aggressors, that they court violence simply by preparing for it, that they are egging on would be purse snatchers and rapists. They unnerve him. When they pass in front of his white '91 Volvo SE Station Wagon they seem to him a potential threat. Because his car does not have power locks, Jack has to check each door individually to double check that it is locked, and he does. It is an old car, bought fifteen years earlier when he and his wife were trying for children. He cannot believe Jasmine lives here.

He never meant to begin seeing her.

On leave to finish a non-existent monograph on an obscure Civil War poet for the past academic year, Jack had not even met her or any one else in her cohort until this fall's Colloquium for the Medieval/Renaissance candidate. By then, she was already a second year doctoral student. Sitting there in the Rare Books section of the library in those uncomfortable metal folding chairs arranged in 10 x 10 rows before the podium, Jack first saw her. That is to say, he saw the back of her head and, when she turned slightly in her chair to allow a fellow student to exit the row, he saw the angle of her face, the curve of her brown cheek, the fall of braids hanging like a sheet between the two sharp points of her shoulders jutting through her gray hoodie.

She was seated in the second row, allowing him to look his fill as he pretended to give his attention to the speaker at the podium. The candidate, a petite brunette, was easily categorized and dismissed. She wore a basic black pants suit, the academic uniform that women in the humanities had long since adopted to give themselves a unisex look and deemphasize their femininity. Every time he went to MLA, he saw these ugly nondescript women. He was not interested in the candidate or her analysis of Margery Kempe. He was a Full Professor and a scholar of Early American Literature. Medievalists held no interest for him anyway—he'd come merely as a show of departmental support—what interested him most was the black girl in the second row with the hair he could not fathom.

Some of the braids followed a pattern like a chain-linked belt he'd seen his wife wear slung low on her hips. Other braids snaked under, over, and between the links, as impossibly complicated as King Minos's labyrinth. Writ on her scalp was the map of his life and all the winding paths it had taken. Laid out like a blueprint, Jack saw his years in graduate school, his first failed job and his subsequent tenure and promotion at his second appointment. Her hair showed him where he was going and where he had been.

Thirty minutes and still no Jasmine.

If he headed for home right now, he'd only be slightly late for dinner. There would be time to pacify Margaret with tales of traffic. Right now, his wife was preparing two separate dinners—a normal one for him and a low-carb, sugar free equivalent for herself.

Jack stood in their vestibule, sorting through their mail.

"Are you home?" his wife called out from the kitchen.

"Yes, I'm home," Jack said, answering the unnecessary question.

So far, none of the mail was for him. He lifted a small yellow envelope. His wife's name showed through the plastic window. He carried ten similar pieces of mail in with him, dropping them onto a pile on the kitchen table. "You have admirers," he said.

"What's that?" Margaret was spooning sugar substitute into a cup of herbal tea.

"The American Vets want you," Jack said. "So do the Hospitalized Vets."

Margaret turned and looked at the growing pile of envelopes. "Oh, that."

All of the surfaces in their kitchen and living room were covered with envelopes addressed to his wife. The coffee table, the end tables, the kitchen table, the top of the television, and two TV trays were covered with pleas from the less fortunate of the world, thanking his wife for her unswerving generosity and beseeching her to bestow it yet again, just one more time, for a cause that really needed it. The American Diabetes Association and the American Heart Association wrote to his wife along with The National Cancer Research Center, the National Association for the Terminally Ill, Feed the Children, the Christian Children's Mission Fund, the North Shore Animal League, a foundation for children who had been born with cleft palates, and a tribe of Hopi Indians. They all asked money from his wife and she gave it freely, her way of mothering the world.

"What kept you?" Margaret asked. Her red hair was fading into strawberry blonde. Her face was pale without makeup; she looked as if she had no eyelashes.

"Traffic."

"Hungry?" she asked. "It's ready."

"I'm sure I could eat," Jack said. He had not thought about food in quite some time, distracted by not having seen Jasmine in two weeks, preoccupied by the suspicion that she was purposely avoiding him. He reviewed a mental outline of his day and realized that he had not eaten in eight hours. Suddenly, he was famished.

He was wrong about the two separate meals. Margaret had made only one, a healthy lasagna made from low-carb noodles, sugar free spaghetti sauce, extra lean ground turkey and low fat mozzarella. They ate in the living room, balancing their plates on their knees since there were no tables upon which they could set their food.

"How is it?"

"Good," Jack said, tunneling through the tasteless meal as quickly as possible. It was like no lasagna he'd ever eaten; the noodles were thin as air, buckling under the weight of cheese and sauce.

"It's good for you, too," she said.

"Is it?"

"Yes. It is."

"Good."

The last time he'd had Italian had been with Jasmine.

He'd arrived at her place early. Jasmine opened the door in a short white terry robe that belted around her waist, her hair wrapped turban style in a fluffy blue towel. Water trickled from her hair down her cheeks. "You're early," Jasmine said. "Dinner's not ready yet."

He'd followed her into the kitchen. Her nimble fingers broke a stack of brittle spaghetti noodles in half and dumped them into a pot of garlic-scented boiling water. "Is spaghetti all right with you?"

He'd wanted to grab her by her shoulders and kiss away the damp spots at the back of her neck where the water had trailed. "Fine with me," he'd said, watching her add a drop of olive oil and stir. "I was once a poor grad student myself."

"Back when dinosaurs roamed the earth?"

"Not *that* long ago."

"Awww." She'd kissed his cheek. "Just a joke."

He was a full hour early and he'd caught her just as she finished washing her hair. When she'd pulled off the towel, a soft damp bush of hair stood out all over her head. Her hair carried the fruity scent of her shampoo and conditioner. She'd tilted her head to the side and roughly dried it.

She'd disappeared down the hallway and into the bathroom. "You're just in time to help me," she'd called back to him.

"Help you what?"

"Tell you in a minute. Why don't you pour us some wine and light the incense?"

Jack poured out cheap wine for them. He'd filled the paper cups and placed them on the edge of the coffee table in front of the couch. He'd lit the small brown cones, releasing the scent of patchouli.

"Here," she'd said when she came back out. "Make yourself use-ful." She held a jar of hair grease. Jack had taken the jar, looking askance at the label featuring the face of an unlikely woman with long silky hair. He'd scanned the capitalized and bolded letters that boasted jojoba, rosemary, nettle, chamomile, coconut oil, and Indian hemp as well as secret African herbs. He'd never seen anything like it. "What should I do?"

"You can oil my scalp," she'd said. "Sit there."

Jack sat on the edge of the couch and Jasmine sat down on the floor in front of him, between his knees. She ran the end of a rattail comb through her hair to divide it into sections. It was his job to make sure that the parts were straight. She sectioned off portions of her thick hair into squares, tiny little boxes of black hair surrounded by pale scalp.

As she'd braided each section, the top of her head had begun to look like an orderly maze. He sat behind her and helped her part the back where she couldn't see. That day he'd been her mirror. He had to hold the portions of hair that she was not working on to keep them from falling into her eyes. He had fistfuls of her hair at his disposal and he didn't know what to do with himself.

They were still early in the relationship and he'd reminded himself why it was wrong, why he would end it soon.

He was much too much older than her.

She was black.

He was married.

She was a grad student.

It didn't matter. All the parts in her hair converged like a map, pointing to her and—against that—none of the reasons would hold.

Jack had taken the comb from her and sank one hand into the portion of her hair that was still damp and unbraided. With the other hand, he'd reached for his wine. He'd drizzled it over her neck and drunk it from the hollow of brown flesh where her neck and collarbone met. "Something on your mind?" Margaret asked.

He wondered where Jasmine was, why she had not gone home, why she was not returning his phone calls. "No."

"I've got something on mine," Margaret said.

"Oh?"

Margaret toyed with her food, twining mozzarella around her fork. Her plate was still half full while his was nearly empty. Jack wondered how it was that he never saw his wife eat, yet she constantly struggled with her weight. "I think we should have a baby."

"Too old," Jack said. "That goes for the both us, by the way."

"You haven't even heard me out," she said. "I didn't mean one of our own." She had been hinting for some time about wanting to raise a Third World baby, to adopt one of the children she'd seen on the feed-the-children commercials. He'd heard it all before. If she couldn't have her own child, she wanted the responsibility of knowing that by helping a child she was helping an entire village. "I'm serious," Margaret said. She straightened her spine and threw her shoulders back. "I would like to adopt a baby of color," she announced.

"There are plenty of those right here in our own country," he reminded her. "Take your pick. Cheaper that way." He took his plate to the kitchen, rinsed it and set it in the dishwasher.

"You are sooo white," Margaret said, twisting her upper lip in such a way that drew attention to the soft downy blonde hair above it, drawing out the word so the way his undergrads did. She said it with a sneer in her voice, as if it were an insult, as if she weren't just as white as he. "Don't make fun. This is important to me."

He tried to escape her in the den where he had one stack of abstracts for an upcoming conference and two stacks of dissertation chapters spread over the couch, but she followed him. Since she could not sit next to him because of the papers, she stalked to the TV and turned it on, pleading her case to the background of *Kojak*.

The children were African, Asian, and South American. Single-handedly his wife wanted to rescue three continents of hungry children. She sounded like the late night paid programming she frequently watched. It was just the price of a cup of coffee and he drank three cups a day. She had a child already picked out. She'd called one of those 800 numbers and they'd sent her three profiles from which to choose. She wanted the little boy, Manolo.

"Would you just look at him?" She held an envelope in her hand and extracted a glossy eight-by-ten photo of the boy and dropped it onto the third chapter of a dissertation on Walt Whitman's novel, *Franklin Evans*. "Here, take a look." Eyes as big as saucers in a brown face peeked out from under long black hair, shaggy as a mop, and stared up at Jack. He couldn't tell if the boy was Indian or South American or Filipino and he was scared to get his wife excited by asking.

She stood by his side, watching him watch Manolo. She rested her hand on his arm, assured. Her touch did nothing for him, though he remembered a time when it could have moved him to tenderness. He tried to hand Manolo back. "Why?" he asked, tired of the whole thing. She wouldn't take the photo, so Jack set it on top of his papers. She knew he hated those begging commercials where overweight has-been actors coddled half-naked bone-thin children. Looking at those children with their big heads and bellies, skeletal limbs and gaunt expressions disturbed him. Why did they always have flies buzzing near them?

"Why?" She repeated his question slowly as if it had been in another language and she'd had to translate. He used to not deny her anything; she used to not have to explain. The envelope dropped from her hand and fell on top of the glossy photo, covering little Manolo's face. Margaret's eyes were bright with unshed tears. "I just want to save something. Honey, can't you see what's happening to us?" she asked, searching his face.

"Nothing's happening," he said. The way he saw it, Margaret had her life and now he had his. He had never complained when she begged out of department functions or was too tired to proofread one of his conference papers, yet had energy enough for *Phil Donahue*, *Oprah*, and telephone conversations that never seemed to end. He no longer reminded her that when they were first married, she would bring him coffee and stay up half the night with him, listening as he rehearsed conference presentations. There had been a time when his wife had been just as excited about his career as he. A time when she dressed carefully for department colloquiums and holiday parties and laughed at ease on his arm.

"Do you think I can't see it?" she asked. "You're leaving me," Margaret said. "And you don't even notice."

Two nights later and Jack was parked once again in front of the Kennedy Fried Chicken, waiting to catch Jasmine. He'd called her from his office and she'd not answered. He'd called her from a payphone and she'd not picked up either. Two weeks without a word from her and he had no idea of what he'd done wrong. He no longer saw her in the copy room or anywhere in the department. He could not imagine why she would not want to see him. They had jargon, the meaning of important words between them. Together, they could talk of hegemony, representation, dichotomy, elision and slippage, terms that Margaret would not understand.

Seemed to him it was just yesterday that Jasmine had pulled him out of his office hours and dragged him to Union Square even though it was snowing. They lined a bench with newspaper for warmth, sat and huddled, the only idiots seated in the park while a stream of people rushed into and out of 14th Street station.

She'd blown on her mocha, rippling the surface of the dark liquid. "I taught the Calamus poems today."

"Ah," Jack had said. "*Homoeroticism*."

She'd made a face. "Please, I don't want to hear that word for the rest of the semester. No one paid any attention once I said it. Half of the class snickered through the entire lecture."

"At the risk of sounding facetious, I must say that I did advise you to leave it off your syllabus."

"I know, I know," she'd said looking into her mocha and not at him. "I had to include those poems. They made me think of us."

"Two men in love?" he'd sputtered. "Us?"

"A secret love that must go unnamed," she'd said. "Us." Beneath her direct and assessing gaze, Jack had felt revered and important, a way he never felt at home. She'd set her drink down. "Give me your hand."

He did as she asked.

"Take off your glove."

"You are aware that it's freezing?"

"Just do it," she'd said. Jack re-wrapped his hot dog in its aluminum foil. Then he'd taken off his glove and given her his hand again. That's the way it was. Though he was the one with tenure, and she a mere slip of a second year grad student with a weakness in theory and rhetoric, and a fondness for overwriting, Jasmine had all the power. She could make him laugh, could make him come, could touch him in a way Margaret never could.

"Now what?" he'd asked.

She'd pulled off her own wool gloves and brought their bare hands together. Like a soothsayer of old, she'd held his palm and explored it with the tips of her fingers. He hadn't known if she was actually reading his palm or merely pretending. He didn't know what she had seen in his hand or what she saw in him at all and it had frightened him. He'd wanted to pull his hand back, in case there had been something in it that could condemn. He didn't want to lose her. His hand had shaken in hers and she'd grasped it with both hands to steady it. Her bare head lowered over his hand, she bent forward, and her braids fell forward too and then resettled, hanging in layers, their ends overlapping at her shoulders. Their ends brushed his palm, searing and burning him.

She'd murmured, "'Not heat flames up and consumes.'"

"Pardon?"

"'Not these, O none of these more than the flames of me, consuming, burning for his love whom I love'. It's Whitman," she said. "You should know that, *professor*." She said *professor* like it was a dirty word and they were in bed with the lights out.

She'd unzipped her down jacket and unbuttoned her shirt, revealing her skin inch by inch, naked above the waist save for a lacy burgundy bra. "'My soul is borne through the open air, wafted in all directions.'"

She'd stopped one button shy of her navel. She'd pulled his naked hand to her throat and collarbone, guiding it downwards until it skimmed the skin above her heart and breasts. The flesh above her heart was warm as his hands explored her. The cold wind had stung his cheeks. Gingerly, he'd reached out and touched the ends of her braids where they hung just above her breasts. They were damp with melting snow; the ends curled under and began to unravel. He'd grabbed a handful of her braids and pulled lightly, using them to bring her mouth to his, feeling nothing that resembled cold.

When they separated, Jasmine had asked, "Will you leave her?"

"Sure," Jack said. Then, because he thought it sounded glib, he'd said, "Yes. If you want me to, I will." He knew that it was what married men always said to the woman on the side in the hopes of appeasing them and continuing the affair, but he'd actually meant it. There was nothing keeping him with Margaret; he'd stayed because—until Jasmine—he hadn't had anywhere else to go, nothing else to do with his life. In his mind, Jasmine was not the woman on the side; Margaret was.

"I don't want you to," Jasmine had said.

To his surprise, he'd found himself standing. He'd sat back down on the bench. "Then I won't," Jack had said, hoping it was the right response. "Okay?"

"Okay," she'd said. "I just wanted to know."

Over an hour now and still no Jasmine. While he waited across the street from her apartment, Margaret was likely wondering where he was. He could see her now, diligently covering the night's uneaten dinner in plastic wrap for him, eating standing by the kitchen sink, looking longingly at the picture of little Manolo while she ate dry cereal in a bowl over the kitchen sink. The bowl, he thought, was unnecessary. Why bother to pour the cereal into a bowl if you weren't going to add milk? It would be just as convenient to tilt the box directly into one's waiting mouth and bypass the middleman. The cereal, he knew, would be low calorie, sugar-free, and fiber-filled. She tried to make him eat that stuff in place of his toasted bagel and cream cheese, but after he'd seen all the parts in Jasmine's hair, Margaret no longer held sway.

Leaning halfway across his seat to double check the lock on the rear right door, he spied Jasmine through the back window, hurrying from the train station. He waited until she made it to her block and he saw her go up her stoop and disappear into her building before he began timing himself. Five minutes should do it. That way, it wouldn't seem as if he'd been sitting out here waiting. That way it wouldn't seem so desperate.

She opened the door, unsurprised to see him. "Let me guess. Just in the neighborhood?"

"Just to see you," Jack said. She motioned him in.

"Is something wrong?"

"You tell me," Jack said. "I haven't seen you in two weeks. I've called, left messages. Didn't you get them?"

"I got them."

He sat down on the couch. "Well?" he said, hating the way he sounded.

"I'm sorry. It's just that I've been busy," she said. "You know, grad school and all. Grading midterms. Trying to get my proposal written before spring break."

"That's all?" he asked.

"That's all."

"So, are we fine?"

"We're fine."

Two hours later, Jack awoke, feeling as if he'd been tricked. Instead of answering his questions, Jasmine had silenced him with sex. He raised himself on his elbow and tried to take a clue from her hair while she slept. With her back to him, he couldn't see her face, couldn't see the small mole above her left eyebrow, or her lips, the upper one brown and the lower one pink. He could only see her hair. It was braided in a simple pattern, one he could tell she had done herself. Cornrows followed the contours of her head and the ends of her braids, hanging down past her shoulders, disappeared into small wooden beads. He didn't know what they might signify, but he didn't trust them.

He nudged her awake.

She turned to face him. "Do you have to go?"

"Not yet," he said. "You changed your hair."

"What?"

"What happened to all of your fancy braids?" he asked, slipping his arm around her.

"Those take hours," she said.

"Do you think I could be a good father?"

"In what sense?"

"My wife wants to have a baby."

She edged out from under the crook of his arm. "How?"

"With me."

Jasmine sat up and propped her back against the headboard. The beads clacked against it, discordant. "I meant, fertility treatments? Surrogacy? Isn't she somewhat old? There might be health concerns and possible complications."

He was expecting something different from her. A little more jealousy, a lot less curiosity. "I'm only three years older than her," he reminded her, feeling old by association. "She wants to adopt."

"You know all those people who bomb abortion clinics? They should all adopt at least one baby. They try to save the ones who aren't even here yet, but they balk at spending tax dollars on the ones already born. Why don't they revamp the foster care system?"

"I'm pro-choice," he reminded her.

"Sorry, I just got a little carried away," Jasmine said. "Adoption is good. I'm going to adopt when I get married."

"It's not a real adoption," he said. "Just one of those programs where you send money." How blithely she spoke of a future without him.

"I don't see what the big deal is if it's just on paper."

It would never be that easy with Margaret. She would want to get to know Manolo. To write and send care packages. She would want to visit, to see his village firsthand. He thought the paper responsibility would not bother him. It was something else entirely. Once—just once—he wanted to be able to tell his wife no and stick to it. He wanted not to give in to her.

"Plenty of things on paper are a big deal," he said, thinking aloud. "Birth certificates. Marriage licenses. The fact that it's on paper doesn't lessen its significance. If anything, it solidifies it." The adoption would be just one more thing to bind he and Margaret, which is what she wanted, hoped for. Young couples did it when their marriage was on the rocks, using babies as glue to mend that which could not be mended. Older couples used pets, adopting dogs and other animals known for their longevity, pretending the pet was a child. Jack's allergies made pets impossible, so Margaret was trying to save their marriage with a monthly donation and a paper adoption. She thought she could finally give him the child they had wanted, give him the family they had desired so long ago, when now all he wanted from her was to be left alone to go his own way, undeterred.

"I just can't do this," Jasmine said. She flicked on the tall halogen lamp by her bed and the sudden light after hours of darkness blinded him, making him blink just to see.

"Did I say something?" he asked.

"No, Jack, it's not what you said. It's who you are." Her eyes made him flinch. There was nothing in them when she looked at him. Just as she had looked at his palm and gone to the heart of him, she now fixed a look on him that went right through him. She had finally seen whatever it was in him that destroyed love.

She picked up her tee shirt from the floor and pulled it on. "You're married; you promised to love somebody else. Somebody not me."

"You told me not to leave her."

"It wasn't real to me yet when I said that. I knew you had a wife, but I just hadn't thought about what that really meant. Then I saw her and I thought—"

"You saw Margaret? Where?"

"I saw a picture of her. Of you both, actually. You know those pictures posted all over Fennimore Lounge, all the old pictures of the Fall Colloquium and the annual holiday party? We were having our monthly American Literature meeting in there and I noticed them for the first time. All these old pictures of faculty and former grad students at department gatherings and I see one of you with your wife. You're holding a small plate with brie and crackers and she's holding your arm and I see her and I think she seems kind, like a woman I could meet in a grocery store and befriend. What right do I have to undermine her? She is a real woman living a real life and she's done no harm to me." He watched her reach for her socks, knowing that each piece of clothing she put on took her farther away from him. Jasmine lifted one knee, balancing on her other foot to pull on her sock. She scooped her boxers up from the floor and stepped into them, as indifferent as if she were dressing in front of a roommate or a mirror. "We're so trite, Jack. The professor and the grad student, what a cliché. It's like something out of a short story. I guess what I'm trying to say is please don't come here anymore."

Except for a quick nod, he didn't respond. He leaned over her side of the bed and turned the light back out. In a minute, he would get dressed and go, but before he did he wanted a moment. From the beginning he had known that sooner than later, it would end. That they would drift, only running into each other occasionally in the hallways between office hours, mingling during department events, pretending to know each other only distantly. Now and again they would meet by accident at different conferences. Perhaps they would sit on a panel together. Over and over again, their lives would run into each other's, quietly intersecting. Yet he had not seen this coming. Her hair had lied.

It seemed just the other day he'd had his hands buried in that crackling bush of hair and her thick and kinky hair had wrapped around his fingers, gnarling them, as impenetrable as the woman herself. It seemed but a minute ago that he was sitting in the Rare Books room, staring at her inscrutable hair and hoping for a chance to get to know her. He reached over the side of the bed and fumbled blindly for his socks.

He let himself into the house. All the lights were off, Margaret already in bed. Jack took off his shoes and padded in his socks to the bedroom. When he slipped into bed beside her, Margaret rolled to him, her face slack with sleep. He wanted to hate her for what had just happened to him. For marrying him. For not being Jasmine. For busying herself in paper causes, behaving as if her world was real and his was not. He wanted to hate her, but it was not her fault. In life, they all had choices to make. He had made his. Was it a mere two days ago that he'd sat in his car and locked the doors to protect himself from a group of harmless women? He had chosen to see them as a threat, chosen not to expose their lie. Instead of waiting for Jasmine, he could have gotten out of his car and followed one of those key-toting women. He could have followed her up the steps to her brownstone and taken her purse despite her precautions, upending it in front of her to show her as she scrambled for her wallet, breath mints, tampons, hand sanitizer and old receipts how uninspired and unimportant were their lives, how— when you came down to it—nothing really mattered.

Jack climbed out of the bed and went down to the den. There he turned on the lights and searched through his stack of papers for that brown envelope and photo. His hand slid over smooth gloss and he picked up the photo of little Manolo. How smug Margaret had been that day, he thought. Inside the envelope he found two more photos. A Venezuelan girl named Isabella smiled at him. He smiled back. The second picture was of a six-year-old Kenyan girl with her hair in cornrows. Rows of braids traveled from her high, wide forehead and convened at the top of her head to form a small braided bun. Her eyes were eyes he'd seen before. The profile said her name was Tzipporah. Tzipporah stared at the camera, unwilling to smile, her face as serious as any adult's. The profile said she lived in the Kwa Vonza village and was a member of the Kamba tribe. Had Jasmine not discarded him, they could have had a little girl just like her.

Jack dug his hand deeper into the envelope, removing an unsigned check, the forms and a pen. Margaret had filled in all of the spaces. He had only to add his signature to hers to make it legitimate. He amended the form before he signed it, substituting Tzipporah for Manolo, making his choice. He signed both documents. He held the paper and check up to the light to examine his scrawl, barely able to recognize his name.

He would work to put this all behind him, but he wouldn't forget her. Every time he had a glass of wine, he'd remember that night in Jasmine's house. Every time he drove through an intersection, he'd remember the patterns in her scalp and how they'd been a map, showing him all the possible ways he could go.

NAVIGATOR OF CULTURE

THAT SUMMER we moved to Bedford-Stuyvesant, I grew four inches, which would have been fine if only I'd been a boy. At twelve, I already towered over my mother at 5'7". The spurt meant I needed new things, none of which my mother could afford in her newly divorced state. "Why couldn't you have done this before we moved out of your father's house?" she asked me several times that summer, each time another item of clothing no longer fit, blaming me as if growing was something I'd done purposely, just for spite. Unbeknownst to me, we'd been living on borrowed time that spring. My parents were only sticking it out until the summer so I could finish my school year without upheaval. As soon as summer came, we moved from the house that I'd always thought of as ours, which was actually only my father's, handed down through generations to him via a thrifty paternal grandmother who'd never liked my mother in the first place.

I spent the summer apologizing for my height, for my sex, for being too young to get my working papers and find a summer job. For my father's affair and his new girlfriend. For the fact that my mother had no skills to fall back on because she'd devoted herself to raising me. The growth spurt did nothing to help my self-confidence. First of all, there was my hair. Sandy-colored, kinky, and comb resistant, my hair was a thick and unruly mass that defied taming. Second, I had braces. Third, I wore glasses which hid what I had been trained to think of as my best asset. My eyes were sometimes brown and sometimes green depending on the light, but no one I knew, except for my mother, ever called them hazel. Folks I knew called them "light eyes," "funny-colored eyes," or just plain "funny eyes." They also used phrases like "high yellow" and "redbone" to describe the color of my skin. As a young girl, I was a list of adjectives representing hundreds of years of social conditioning. I was awkward and shy, tall for my age, and as bony-kneed as a giraffe, but because of the eyes and skin, people assured me I'd grow into being a real looker. Until then, I was merely a financial hardship.

My mother assured me that everything would turn out all right once the divorce was settled and the child support kicked in. Until then, there was only what we had and I had outgrown much of it. We were not poor, but we were dislocated and dispossessed. This state of being, my mother told me, would pass. It was temporary, just like our new neighborhood. The night we moved in, I'd rushed to unroll and tape my favorite posters to the wall, but my mother stopped me, warning, "Don't get attached."

With nothing to be done about my boyish height, my mother waged war on my hair. Were it not for our newly impoverished state, which deemed visits to the beauty parlor an unaffordable extravagance, my mother would have never taken me to Miss Jefferson. A statuesque woman of indeterminable age, Miss Jefferson did hair to supplement her social security income. She seemed old enough to be my grandmother, but everyone called her Miss and never Mrs. Her own hair was jet black and she wore flamboyant hats, even when at home. Her apartment was always filled with a crowd of women in various states of preparation. They sat under dryers, balancing plates of food on their knees. They smoked at her kitchen table, blowing wreaths through the window grates, their heads coiffed in shower caps and rollers. They dawdled in the living room by the record player with their shoes off, and their feet carefree. They lingered at Miss Jefferson's—some with their hair done, some with it freshly washed and knotty—talking and laughing uncensored even in the presence of children.

These women made my mother dreadfully uncomfortable. The first time she brought me, she didn't touch anything. She didn't accept a glass of water or soda. She didn't even sit down. Right before I reached for the metal doorknocker, my mother grabbed me back to her. Said, "Remember that these women are not the kind you ever want to be."

Miss Jefferson opened the door wearing a royal blue hat with a curving brim that reminded me of the women in my father's church, which we no longer attended. "Well Rita, come to get Hazel's hair done? Johnnie Mae said you'd probably be by."

"Yes," my mother said, smiling in apology. "Hazel's hair is so difficult to work with."

Miss Jefferson ran a hand over my hair, but made no comment. "How you been getting on?"

"Well, thank you," my mother answered, gingerly stepping inside. "And yourself?"

"I'm about as good as I'm gonna get. Can I get you anything?" Miss Jefferson asked. "I cooked earlier. There's plenty to eat and drink."

"Oh no, thank you anyway. I'm not really hungry." Her eyes said she would never be that hungry. "*She's* eaten already, too."

"Have a seat. Make yourself comfortable. I'm sure you haven't met a lot of the people since you're new. Mostly everybody in here lives on this block."

"Actually, I really have to be going. I have a few things to do, errands to run."

This was news to me, as I'd not seen my mother do one productive thing since our move. Whenever I'd run inside for lunch, I'd find my mother—still in her slip, never having dressed for the day—slumped in front of the television watching reruns of *Gidget* and *Fantasy Island*.

When she did leave the house, she spoke to no one, snubbing the wom-en on the block outside on their stoops watching infants, keeping an eye on older children and shooting the breeze. She sneered at their presence, and told me they were nothing but welfare queens. In any case, I never saw any furs or Cadillacs. "What errands?" I asked.

My mother squeezed my fingers so tight I thought they would snap. "Just errands, dear." She looked at her watch, a slender bangle of gold with a tiny face that cost more than Miss Jefferson's entire living room set.

Miss Jefferson looked down at the watch, too. "She'll be ready by six."

My mother pushed money into my hand and told me to behave.

As soon as she left, I let out a breath I hadn't known I'd been hold-ing. Then Miss Jefferson spoke so only I could hear her, "I think your mother is a little too busy to drag you over here every other week. Women like her have a million things to do. After I finish your head and you get home, make sure and tell her that she don't have to bring you over here no more." She adjusted the brim of her hat. "Besides you're old enough that you can come down here by yourself. How's that sound?"

"Yes," I said quickly, feeling something unfurl inside of me. I had been forgiven for my mother.

Miss Jefferson's apartment became my refuge that summer. There I could sit and listen in on the women. I could play with her granddaugh-ter Annette who, for some reason, lived with Miss Jefferson instead of her own mother. Miss Jefferson let me hear things I wasn't supposed to hear until I was years older and eat things that were no good for me. In Miss Jefferson's kitchen, where all the women concurred, I began to believe that my mother was the anomaly, the strange one. My mother never left sugar in the bag it came in. She always poured it into a jar. She always kept our bread in a box and she never reused our cooking oil or kept it in an emptied can of Crisco. She used baking soda only to keep the refrigerator and drains smelling fresh, never for brushing teeth when the toothpaste ran out. My mother was not one to ever let the toothpaste run out.

Fifteen summers later, and I have come back to Bedford-Stuyvesant a stranger. The streets in Bed-Stuy have all new names and I get lost twice before I find the one I want. Cautiously, I approach my old block, slowing before nearing the children at the hydrant splashing oncoming cars. I park two doors down from where Miss Jefferson's should be. Six young boys on her stoop eye my car. Despite their poverty, they are dressed in expensive and oversized clothing. They are boys without a pot to piss in or a window to throw it out of, the type of boys who make me wish I had *The Club* for my car.

The sidewalk is cracked in too many places to count. I step—carefully—around the sections of dirt and weeds that sprout between the broken concrete. "Excuse me," I say, but no one moves aside to let me up the stoop. Instead I have to navigate, wending my way through their space, squeezing around the bodies of these young black boys. Briefly, I consider getting back in my car and heading home. "These are your own people," I whisper, reminding myself.

I knock on Miss Jefferson's door. The peephole cover slides back into place, and a woman's voice comes through loud and clear. "We're not interested."

The voice is much younger than Miss Jefferson's. "I'm not selling anything," I say. "I'm looking for Miss Jefferson. Does she still live here?"

Locks click and turn. A young woman opens the door as far as the safety chain will allow. "What do you want with my grandmother?"

I see an eye, half a face, an arm, a hand. "Annette?"

"Yes," she says, making no move to take off the safety chain.

"It's me Hazel," I say. "I used to live on this street. Don't you remember me?"

The door closes and reopens sans chain.

Annette steps back and lets me in. We eye each other uncomfortably, superimposing our current images over the ones we remembered.

"What happened to your glasses?" I blurt.

As a child Annette had worn glasses—thick lenses and cheap frames—the only kind that Medicaid would cover, the only kind that Miss Jefferson could afford. She was always there whenever I came to get my hair pressed and curled, sitting in a corner, brushing her one doll's hair. Although she did everyone else's hair on the block, Miss Jefferson never pressed Annette's. At twelve, Annette had been the only girl still in pigtails. The woman standing before me now wears stylish double-strand twists. Annette had been my first friend when I moved onto the block. Though I have grown, matured, and changed, I never thought she too would do the same.

"I got contacts," she says. "What about your braces?"

"I got them off," I say, feeling an urge to cover my teeth with my lips.

"So, Hazel, what brings you by? It's been a long time."

"I was in the neighborhood, so I thought I'd drop by and see how Miss Jefferson was doing. So how is she?"

"She's not getting any younger and old age is taking its toll on her."

"I'm so sorry." I follow Annette through the living room and towards the kitchen. The living room looks completely unlived in. Gone are the extra folding chairs placed all around for customers. Gone are the bonnet style hair dryers propped on top of tables. Gone are the women, the voices, the smoke. "This place used to be jam-packed."

"It's been a while," Annette says. Groceries sit in plastic bags on the kitchen table. Annette begins to pull out cans with no frills labels.

"How've you been?" she asks.

"Fine," I say. "You?"

"Good. Want something to drink?"

"Water will be fine."

"It's not bottled," Annette says, taking a glass from the cupboard and pouring cold water into it over a sink filled with dirty dishes. "This okay?"

"It's fine." I take the glass and sip cautiously. I do not drink tap water. "Thanks."

Annette asks questions without looking up from her unpacking. Cans of peas, mixed vegetables, peaches, and fruit cocktail pile on the table. "You married?"

"Yes. Three years," I say, wondering why we are talking like this. Instinctively, I do not mention that my husband is white. "You?"

"With two kids. Both girls," she says. "Guess you went to college."

"Yes," I say, wondering if I should apologize for it. "What do you do?"

"Hair."

"Just like your grandmother." I join Annette at the counter and hand her cans to stock the cupboards.

"I'm licensed," Annette says. "I don't work out of my kitchen. I've got a shop in Jersey."

I'd always thought of hair as something done in basements and kitchens to the backdrop of daytime soap operas. "I didn't mean anything," I say.

Annette turns to me. "Catching up with you has been priceless Hazel, but I'd like to know why you're really here."

"I already told you."

"You and I both know that you were not just *in the neighborhood*," she says. Her glance sweeps over me. "From the looks of it, you haven't been *in the neighborhood* for years."

"What's that supposed to mean?"

"If you'd been *in the neighborhood*, then you would know," she said.

Holding a can of pear halves, she eyes me with pity and condescension. "For your own self-respect, Hazel, please tell me you're not here to fulfill some sort of nostalgic wish to get your hair done like you used to when you were a little girl."

I play with the label on a can of peas, prying it from its overlapping adhesive seal, ignoring Annette's condescension. "It's not the way you make it sound. I didn't come here for my hair, but I did come to see your grandmother."

"If not for your hair, then for what?"

I don't know how to tell her the real reason. Annette makes me uncomfortable in Miss Jefferson's kitchen, though nothing about the kitchen itself has changed in fifteen years. Not even the kitchen table with its peeling padded chairs. Nothing except for Annette and myself. We are too different now. No longer girls of twelve, no longer best friends, we are two women with only Miss Jefferson in common and I have come to claim my part of her. I want her to advise me. I want to know where I belong, to know what I am doing and I want that feeling to come as easy as turning in this kitchen, and opening a cupboard and finding exactly what I want just where I thought it would be. "I just need to see her, that's all. I don't owe you any explanations."

"You never even said good-bye to me, Hazel. Johnnie Mae was the one who told us you all had moved," Annette says, her eyes watering. She closes the cupboard doors. "Her room is the last one on the left."

No one answers when I knock. I push open the bedroom door and enter. "Hi, Miss Jefferson. It's me, Hazel," I say, coming close to the bed. Miss Jefferson is propped up in the bed behind six sagging pillows, simultaneously watching the television and listening to the radio. She has lost weight, at least thirty pounds, and now seems a waifish shrunken version of her former self. Her black hair—now wispy, braided and pinned back—has gone completely gray.

Miss Jefferson raises rheumy eyes. "Nettie?"

"No, it's Hazel," I say, drawing my name out. "*Hazel*. I came by today to see you."

Miss Jefferson smiles and pats my hand. "Nettie, when you gonna call those people and have them turn the heat on? A body could freeze to death in here. It feels like the dead of winter."

It is hotter than July in her room. The windows are closed and a small box fan circulates stale air. I kneel by the bed. "No, it's not Annette. Miss Jefferson, it's me, Hazel. I used to live up the block and you used to do my hair when I was a little girl," I say.

"Tell them I pay good money and if I have to I'll start deducting from the rent."

"Miss Jefferson, you don't understand—"

"It's not right for them to treat me like this," Miss Jefferson says. "They think we don't know nothing and won't stand up for our rights. I'll fix them."

"You're right. It's not fair," I agree. I want to talk to her, but there is no use. I need to talk to someone I trust and I trust Miss Jefferson more than my own mother, but the sharp woman I remember is gone. I'd been counting on her. I'd thought surely Miss Jefferson would have the answers.

Sometimes now, after seeing my husband off, I go back upstairs to take off my clothing and look at myself. I undress, as if coming home from a hard day at work. Undress as if I have not just spent the last hour and fifteen minutes showering, cleansing, toning, and moisturizing in preparation of starting my day. Undress and stand naked in the mirror on the other side of our bedroom door. Face away from the mirror and twist so I can see myself from the back. Stand to the side, skimming my hands over my stomach and hips. Face myself and look at my breasts, holding each one tenderly, wincing even though there is never any pain. Soon enough, they'll be sore and I want to be ready. My body is changing even though I can't actually see the signs yet. The changes are subtle and slow to come just now, but soon there'll be a snowball effect and I know I'll wake up one morning visibly pregnant. Then I'll have to tell my husband and once I tell him, it will all have to be real.

The thing is, I don't feel like a woman having a baby. I don't feel like anything but my normal self. I don't feel all of the things I'm supposed to feel. All I can think about are all the changes we'll have to make, all of the adjustments. My husband will be overjoyed. A baby right now will fit perfectly into his schedule. He has these five, ten and fifteen year plans for our life together. His forethought is one of the things I love most about him, but I'm scared to take this step. With the exception of the one brief summer in Bedford-Stuyvesant, my life has never strayed from the course my mother set it on. College, graduate school, marriage and a home on Long Island, and now pregnancy—all of the steps of adulthood I've had to navigate. I've followed every step faithfully yet I feel as though I've lost my way. This pregnancy feels like a turning point, like once I give this baby life, I will wake up and find I've become my mother. I know I'm not supposed to feel like this, but I don't know what to do about it or how to make that feeling go away. I want Miss Jefferson to redirect me, to tell me this is a normal part of the process, that I am just going through a phase and that everything will turn out all right.

For years, I have clung to the memory of Annette's grandmother and her simple acceptance. For years, I have remembered the feel of those long fingers lathering my hair and kneading my scalp over her kitchen sink. Now I lean in close to Miss Jefferson, smelling the fetid breath of dentures that have been soaked but not brushed. Miss Jefferson is completely unaware of her surroundings and the long fingers that have scratched my scalp are now gnarled and veiny.

"You'll tell them for me, right?" Miss Jefferson asks.

"I will," I say.

"That's my good girl. You're a good girl," Miss Jefferson says, patting my arm. "Always have been."

Annette waits for me in the hallway and we walk back to the kitchen.

"She's gone gray." I sit down at the kitchen table. Annette fills the kitchen sink with water and squirts dishwashing liquid over the dishes.

"No, she just stopped dyeing it," Annette says. She looks at me in disbelief. "You didn't know?"

I hadn't even suspected. "Annette, is she all right? She seemed...I don't know. Does she have Alzheimer's?"

"It's just old age, Hazel."

"Are you sure?"

"She doesn't wander out in the street in her pajamas or forget where she lives. She remembers when she wants to. She's got her wits about her."

"Who takes care of her?"

"I guess you can say I do, even though she lives alone now. I cook for her, do the shopping, bring her food. I come and wash all the dishes she piles up, then I cook for her so she can dirty them again."

"You know, I used to wish Miss Jefferson was my mother."

"My grandmother has that effect on people. Every little girl that came in here wanted to steal my Nana."

And here I thought that I had been special. "What are you going to do with her?"

"Do?"

"Don't you think she needs full-time care? Look, if it's about money—"

Annette drops the pan she's been scrubbing back into the water. "What? You'll come in and save the day? Hazel, she doesn't want to go anywhere. This is her home. She's not bothering anybody, sitting in her room watching TV. I can afford to put her in a home if I wanted to do that to her, but I don't. The people on this block love her and know her. She doesn't want to move in with me and my family. She doesn't want to go to an old folk's home and live with strangers. She wants to be here."

"I just thought—"

"I know what you thought." Annette turns the water off and wipes her wet hands on her slacks. She walks me to the door. "Same ole Hazel."

"What did I ever do to you?"

"You know, even when we used to play dolls, you had your nose stuck high in the air," Annette says before she closes the door in my face.

I stand outside Miss Jefferson's apartment. "I don't know what you're talking about," I tell the closed door. "And neither do you."

Of course, I am lying.

Here we are in Miss Jefferson's apartment: We head for Annette's bedroom, making our way through all of the women waiting to get their hair done. I bring a few of my dolls over in a shiny pink plastic traveling case that holds them and their accessories. Annette's doll lives in a shoebox. She opens the lid and pulls out an eleven and a half inch Christie, Barbie's black friend. Not until 1980 would Mattel call one of its black dolls Barbie. The first black Barbie wears a red sequined showgirl outfit and open-toed red mules made of sturdy plastic. She has a short, curly Afro and long dangly gold earrings. Both of her arms are bent at the elbows. One hand in her hair, the other resting against her hip, she is all come hither. But this is not her. This is Christie, just one of Barbie's many friends, like Midge and PJ. I have more than thirty Barbies and none of them are black, so I know.

Later, I would learn that Miss Jefferson refused to let Annette own white dolls, but then I was scornful and unimpressed. Apparently, my mother never considered that surrounding a little black girl like me with white dolls who looked nothing like me would encourage me to hate myself and make me wish I could be them instead of me. Unlike Miss Jefferson, my mother didn't believe dolls influenced self-image and standards of beauty. Neither she nor I knew anything of the damage being done to me.

"Don't you have any real Barbies?" I ask.

"In your hand," Annette says.

"No," I say, shaking my head sadly, a jeweler informing a customer that the diamond brought in is a fake, just an eight-sided waste of glass and reflected light. "Not a Christie. A Barbie."

"That is Barbie," Annette says.

"Barbie's white. But your doll is pretty anyway. She reminds me of my mother."

"Your mother?"

"My mom has hair like that."

Annette takes the doll out of my hands and fingers the long silky hair. "Don't you see how raggedy the women who come in here look before my Nana fixes their hair all nice? Your mother's hair looks just like theirs before she gets it done."

"You're wrong; my mother has good hair."

"Yeah, good and nappy!"

I snatch the plastic Christie from Annette and hold my thumb just under her neck. I squeeze until her head pops off and the plastic rotator rolls under a chair.

If I were Annette, I'd hate me too. Never once did I think to replace the doll I'd decapitated. It never crossed my mind that Annette had nothing else to play with since I'd destroyed her one and only doll. It never even occurred to me to say sorry.

I get out of the car and head back to Miss Jefferson's. I knock on the apartment door. The peephole cover moves and I know Annette is watching me. I imagine that she sees my contrition. I imagine she is laughing. I knock and knock again, but the cover slides back into place, shutting me from her sight.

We lived in Bed-Stuy for only one summer. By the time the next school year began, we had a brownstone in Park Slope and my mother had enough money in child support to send me to private school. Each day, I rode the subway to the Upper East Side of Manhattan, moving further and further away from the neighborhood and the people my mother had warned me away from. By the time the next summer rolled around, though we both lived in Brooklyn, the distance between me and Annette seemed miles and miles away.

Back in my car, I hesitate before pulling out onto the street. I sit with the doors locked and try to get my bearings, wishing I had never come. Lost and disoriented, I try to remember which way will take me back home, unsure of how I can ever get home from here.

BEEN MEANING TO SAY

LESLIE SINGLETON awoke to the unexpected drone of a lawnmower. It was late November and he and his neighbors had long since stopped cutting the grass. He'd fallen asleep on the couch again and, as he rose, a cramp stiffened his neck. With Iphigenia now gone, no one threw bedspreads over him, nudged his shoes off, slipped pillows under him, or did anything to make him more comfortable. The remote was on his lap, the *Philadelphia Inquirer* was folded on the end table by his side and the TV was on, but he couldn't remember what he'd been watching before he'd fallen asleep. Now, without Iphigenia, such a simple thing as that had become difficult for him to do.

Joey Leibert was outside in the neighboring yard doing the edges with his cordless grass trimmer. Every so often, he'd get too close and the line of cord would slap against the metal stake of the fence and he'd have to bump the feed head to continue.

"You're either too early or you're too late," Leslie called, standing between his open door and screen door.

The lanky white man looked around for the voice. When he saw Leslie, he waved. "How ya doing Mr. Singleton? Just giving her a little trim." He switched off the trimmer.

"You should let the lawn alone, Joey. It'll be snowing soon enough."

"The agent's bringing a family by tomorrow. I wanna make it look nice for them." He winked. "With any luck, this will be my last time."

"They're going to look at a house on Thanksgiving?"

"That's the plan."

"Good family?" Leslie asked.

Joey Leibert shrugged. "If they've got the down payment, they're good enough for me."

Leslie laughed with him. "How's your Ma doing?"

Joey Leibert kicked at the guard protector to knock stray cuttings loose. "She's great. Just great."

"How's she like the place?"

"Oh, she likes it just fine." Joey Leibert raked the yard. "She won't have to worry about maneuvering up and down these steps come winter. That can be real hard on the knees when you get to be old."

Leslie tapped his leg and smiled grimly. "I know."

"Come on, Mr. Singleton. You're not that old."

"Getting there."

"Your Carole's years behind me. How's she doing anyway?"

"Coming for Thanksgiving. Bringing the husband and the boy."

"Hah," Joey said. "Sounds like you're all set."

The phone rang inside and Leslie excused himself to Mrs. Leibert's son, which was how he always thought of Joey, even after all this time.

They could not possibly come and stay with him for the short break, his daughter said. Carole spoke to him in a no nonsense voice, as if she were talking to one of her undergrads and not her own father. She was on her cellular phone and Leslie wanted her signal to go in and out as it sometimes did so he would lose the last of her words.

It cut him that she would spend the holidays with her husband's family and not him. Especially when she'd promised. He remembered it clearly. A week after the funeral, she'd called to check on him. When he heard her voice, so like her mother's, he'd started to weep into the phone. It was then that she'd promised to bring the family to stay with him for the Thanksgiving break, her way of soothing a grieving old man. It was May then, and she'd had to cancel her students' finals and give them take-homes in order to be in Philadelphia for the wake and funeral. She and her husband were sending their son to camp for the summer since they had gotten some sort of grant to do research in some sort of humanities center. She'd given him some long story about junior faculty productivity and procuring tenure which was supposed to explain why he wouldn't see any of them that summer. Their next break was Thanksgiving and she'd promised she'd bring her family to stay and it would be just like old times, except without Iphigenia. Now she said she couldn't stay, but they might drop by for a few hours on Thanksgiving Day, which wasn't the same at all.

He told her so.

She said, "Dad, you have to be reasonable. Martin's parents—"

"—Is it because—" He had cut her off, but he couldn't continue, couldn't say the words.

"Because what, Dad?"

"Just give me the truth. Why don't you just say it?"

"Say what?" she asked. Then: "Fine. It's not the same anymore with Mom gone. We really don't want to stay the night."

"Why?" he asked her.

Never one to pull punches, his daughter said, "I don't want my son growing up like I did," she said.

"What was wrong with your childhood, honey?" he asked, wondering if he'd ever left her alone with an uncle or male cousin.

"You were."

"Me?" he said. "Me?"

"Don't act so surprised, Dad. You. Yes, you and your attitude."

"Attitude?"

"Are you going to repeat everything I say? Amir, leave that alone honey before you break it," he heard her say. "Fine. Then put it in the trunk for Mommy, okay? Thank you. Martin, take that away from him." Then she was back again. "Dad, you've always been very unapproachable. Mom was always there to smooth things over after you'd fluffed them. Mom always had to pick up the slack. She had to do extra just to make up for you. Now there's no one to cover for you."

"It wasn't like that," he said.

"I call them like I see them, Dad," she said. "I was there too, you know. Excuse me a second, Dad. Amir—" He heard the sounds of traffic before she placed the phone against something so he couldn't hear her.

He never thought of himself as having deficiencies or of his wife having to compensate for them. Not his Iphigenia. She was just a loving and generous woman. A keeper of the peace. It was in her nature to make things right.

Everything began and ended with Iphigenia. It took Leslie almost three years of marriage to her before he got up the courage to ask her about her name. He'd thought it an uncommon name, especially for a black woman born in the 1930's. Before her, he'd met his share of Esthers and Eunettas, Anna Maes and Audreys, Marians and Mabels, names that were old-fashioned even back then. His good buddy Roland had set him up on his first date with Iphigenia. Leslie had never before met an Iphigenia and he'd been impressed before he'd even seen her legs. It wasn't every day a man met a woman with a name like that and he strove to be worthy of her. He'd made a vow to himself that he would not become one of those husbands who shortened his wife's name out of convenience. He would preserve his wife's name in its entirety, never referring to her as Ginny or anything other than Iphigenia.

Iphigenia, sacrificed for favorable winds.

"I'm back," Carole said.

"Can you at least let the boy stay over, even if it's just one night?"

"Dad, the boy is my son. His name is Amir."

"I can't remember all the time."

"There's nothing wrong with your memory. You just don't want to say his name and give my son the respect he deserves. Maybe it would be better for us not to come."

"Respect? Since when do eight-year-olds get respected? Besides I just don't like saying those Mumbo Jumbo names."

"It is not a Mumbo Jumbo name, Dad. It's Arabic. It means prince. Ruler. We've gone over this before."

Arabic or not, Leslie thought his grandson's name sounded just as silly as the names he'd been hearing slapped on children lately. It seemed that every time he turned around, children were being named after cars, medicines and condiments. "Neither you or Martin is Muslim. Why's he need an Arabic name?"

"We wanted something with meaning. Something that reflected our pride in our African heritage and culture."

The way he saw it, Carole was a generation too late for names with meanings. Her generation had gotten all of the real African or Arabic names. Iphigenia had wanted Carole to be named Naima because it meant tranquil and benevolent. Naima sounded too much like Naomi to him and Naomi sounded too much like somebody whining. So they named her Carole since she was born on Christmas Eve. It seemed to him that the generation that had purposefully chosen African and Arabic names as symbols of pride had given way to a newer generation of illiterate parents willing to slap anything on a child and call it a name. It wasn't safe to have a meaningful name anymore. People were liable to confuse the meaningful and the made-up.

"Meaning," Leslie said. "Not something like Carole, you mean. I guess being named after the birthday of our Lord Jesus Christ can't compare to being a Muslim prince."

His daughter sighed as if she'd been waiting for him to say exactly that. "And you wonder why I'm not bringing him over?"

Leslie went back outside after Carole hung up, but Mrs. Leibert's son was already gone. The Leibert's lawn was short and manicured now, no ragged edges, no unsightly exterior to warn away a prospective buyer.

Overbrook was still a good neighborhood. The Leiberts in the twin next door were the last white family to move off the block. Mrs. Leibert had been having trouble making it up and down the stairs for four years before her son the pharmacist finally convinced her to move into an assisted living facility. For three months Leslie had been watching the agents and potential buyers go in and out of Mrs. Leibert's house. The Leiberts had been living there when he and Iphigenia first moved in, long before they ever had Carole. He'd never been inside, but he could guess at the peeling paint on the bathroom's water-stained ceiling, the old white tile, the Formica kitchen, the living room's wood paneled walls identical to the inside of his house. The Leibert's son Joey was a full ten years older than his own Carole. Joey was a good boy, even though he had moved his mother out of the only house she'd ever known. He'd come every other Sunday afternoon to mow the little patch of grass in front of the house, and twice a week in the winter to shovel the snow and salt the steps. In the fall, he'd bag the fallen leaves and set them on the curb. Still, it must have been a lot for a man to do when he had his own family and his own leaves and his own grass and his own snow, his own seasons to cultivate and his own winter to beat back with the force of his shovel.

With Iphigenia there, their house had pleased him. The slow deterioration of it had gone noticed but ridiculed. The paint on the ceiling was chipping and the windows needed new caulking, but who had time for those things? It was hard work, keeping a house. Things had a way of slipping through, coming undone. They were too busy getting on with the business of life. They put off the household repairs to take a line-dancing class. To have friends over for Bid Whist, then a few hands of pinochle. Now, with Iphigenia gone, he did none of those things alone and the house mocked him. It had never been the money so much as the time. You needed time to fix a house. Time to let someone come in and do the work. With Iphigenia around he'd had none. Now he had more time than he could stand. No longer could he pretend the house's disrepair was the sign of a busy and happy couple rather than that of an old man himself in need of repairs.

Soon, in the seasons to come, he'd have to pay a stranger for his upkeep. There would be no one to trim his grass and rake his leaves when he could no longer do it himself. Leslie didn't have a Joey. He only had a Carole.

Back in the kitchen, Leslie placed a frozen turkey in a basin of cold water and hoped it would thaw in time. Iphigenia had always made the Thanksgiving dinner, but he had been willing to try. He would have split the wishbone with his grandson, pretending to have no strength so the boy would pull off the larger part.

He wasn't asking for much. They wouldn't even have had to spend that much time with him. Everyone would have had their own room. As always, there were the three bedrooms upstairs. His and Iphigenia's master bedroom at the front of the house, above the enclosed porch. Carole's room at the back of the house, over the kitchen and mudroom. The middle room, smallest of all three. It had never belonged to anyone, but slowly, over the years, Iphigenia had come to claim it for herself. She'd had the reclining chair brought up there. He didn't remember getting it up the stairs but somehow he must have because it was there, right by the radiator just like she'd wanted it. She'd had him put her console sewing machine in there, too, though she kept the machine folded under so the whole thing looked like a small table. She'd used it as a place upon which to set down her drinks and reading glasses. The room was cluttered with things that had meaning only to her and, except for the slippers, he'd left it exactly as it had been the last time she'd sat in the recliner, the night he'd found her dead.

He would have given the boy Iphigenia's room. There was no bed in there, but there was a serviceable cot in the basement that he could have brought up. He'd have liked it, Leslie knew. Though small, the room was inviting.

Those slippers were the only things he'd disturbed. Her very last pair of house slippers. He'd bought them for her so she'd stop wearing his. His were dark leather, with strips that crisscrossed over the toes, the kind you could buy in any discount store. His Iphigenia would slip into his too large slippers and wear them all through the house, the backs flapping along the floor without the weight of a man's heels to ground them.

Leslie waited a month after she died before he took the slippers from the middle room. Carrying them one in each hand as if to prevent each slipper from knowing its fate, he brought them into the master bedroom. He knelt by Iphigenia's side of the bed and placed them there. There they waited. She needed only to return, slide out of bed and slip right back into them.

They were God-awful ridiculous looking slippers. Boudoir slippers made of lavender satin with short heels and a bit of fluff across the bridge of the toes. The kind of slippers women wore in the movies he'd grown up watching. Women with thinly drawn eyebrows and shoulder-length beveled curls and Cupid's Bow mouths. Women who owned vanity tables and silver-backed brushes. Women clad in long silky negligees with matching robes with fur at the collar and cuffs. And slippers. Women wearing the daintiest matching slippers. Those lavender slippers had cost him thirty-eight dollars before tax, eight times the price of his own and Iphigenia hadn't even liked them. She pretended she did, but he had known by the half-hearted way she'd pranced when she modeled them. He could still hear her forced enthusiasm, "Look at me. Dorothy Dandridge! Ms. Lena Horne! Watch out, Greta Garbo! Move over Lauren Bacall."

Loneliness was inevitable without her. He missed his wife, to be sure. Her presence and smell and the way she never rolled her hair at night tight enough to keep the small hard pink and yellow rollers from slipping off and rolling under him. He missed getting up to close the window because she'd gone to sleep with it open even though he warned her about catching colds. He missed the way she said "Mmmhmm" right before going to sleep, knowing it meant *I love you*. He missed working with her. Arguing over their daughter's faults. Iphigenia thought Carole could do no wrong, but he thought she'd outgrown them, relying too much on what was in a book rather than what she knew to be so. She believed anything she read and now that she was a professor at a college he'd never heard of she got paid to read more of those books and write articles about what she'd read.

Whenever he and Carole argued, Iphigenia had been there to smooth things over, to keep the peace. To remind them that the reason they quarreled was because their temperaments were so similar. "Headstrong," she'd say. "The both of you are just two mules and I've got all the carrots."

Maybe Carole was right. Iphigenia had been sacrificing herself a little each day to smooth his way over and keep his paths clear. Maybe that was why she passed away before him. Perhaps she had just grown tired of looking after him. He'd always thought he'd be the first to go.

More than anything he missed her being there with him, missed the presence of a spouse, missed having her know him well and being there so that he could turn to her and say, "Isn't that right?"

They'd gotten spoiled, he and Iphigenia. They'd had only each other for so long that he sometimes thought of their daughter as a presence intruding upon he and his wife's routine. They'd been childless for fourteen years before Carole came along, so it was hard not to think of Iphigenia as someone he had all to himself. He was old enough to be his daughter's grandfather. Maybe they had left Carole out. They'd been so used to just each other for so long that, once their daughter came along, they didn't know what to do with her. He'd treated her like a guest, a relative come to stay just until she could get back on her feet again, the way Carole didn't want her son to be treated.

He could try, but he could not promise. There were times when he would look at his grandson and think what a fine boy he was, sometimes even getting teary enough to wish he could live to see the boy graduate college. There had been times when he and the boy would be in the living room together and he would mean to reach out for him, to encourage him or pat his shoulder, but as often as he thought it, Leslie stayed in his chair and watched the boy playing on the carpet, running his truck around in circles in the area between the TV and the coffee table. He spoke only when the boy did things he thought children ought not do. "Back up some from the TV," he'd say. "You're going to strain your eyes like that." Not what he'd been meaning to say at all.

He'd call his daughter and apologize. He'd cook Thanksgiving dinner anyway and hope to convince her to bring her husband and the boy. They could go back to Martin's parents' house afterwards. All he wanted was a little time with them.

Carole didn't answer. His call went straight to the voice mail. He wondered if she'd turned off her phone just so she wouldn't have to speak to him. "Carole honey, it's Dad. I'm sorry about what I said. I didn't mean any of it and if you bring your family over tomorrow I promise I'll try and do better. All right, that's all I have to say. 'Bye now. Hope to see you real soon."

Leslie put the bird in the oven early the next morning, not trusting the instructions on the plastic. He made the stuffing on top of the stove. He made the stuffing from a box and got his string beans and cranberry sauce from cans. His biscuits he'd bought frozen. There would be no pies and he had never liked collard greens.

He had been watching the parade on TV when he heard a car door slam outside his house. He looked out of the enclosed porch's window, but it wasn't Carole. A white woman and a black family emerged from the car.

The couple dressed neutrally, casually, the way they'd probably learned to dress in case the owners were at home and not as well-to-do. Their clothes were unlabeled and understated, yet expensive. The woman's dreadlocks were a lighter shade of brown than the unlocked hair at her scalp; the man was bald. They each carried a young child, but Leslie couldn't tell if the children were twins or not.

The agent entered the code into the lockbox and removed the key. She opened the screen door, unlocked the front door and motioned them to enter. Before they did, the woman re-clipped her daughter's barrette and kissed the top of the little girl's head. The husband followed after his wife, pretending to bump the daughter he carried against the door's frame. The girl's surprised giggle followed the family into the house, where Leslie could not see them.

There inside, the agent would convince them.

Don't buy it! Leslie wanted to shout. Not just because you have those children and you think this is a better environment for them to grow up in. Not just so they can play safely in their own yards. Not just to keep them from the riff raff. Don't buy this house for them. They will grow up and they will leave it. They will leave you. They will scorn what you have saved for. They will want apartment complexes with personal parking spaces. They will not want to wake up each day and set garbage cans out on the street just to protect their parking spaces until they get home. They will want central air. Hardwood floors will not move them. Once they are no longer children they will not find joy in sliding across a waxed floor in their socks, pretending that they are ice-skating. Instead they will want to cover up that floor with thick, plush carpet. Your son will say Berber like it's the name of his mistress. Your daughter will shop for fixtures the way your wife shopped for lingerie.

He did not wait for them to return to their car. He will meet them after closing. After they reach settlement, he will see them slowly moving in. He will wend his way around their two daughters who will not keep to their side of the steps. He will see them when he comes out to sweep his front yard clear of the snack bags and straw wrappers their daughters leave behind them when they go down the block to jump rope. By that time, they will see in him only an old man, crotchety and disgruntled, bothered by the smallest things, unvisited and alone.

Maybe his daughter will make friends with the wife. Maybe his family and their family will smile at each other over their grills, folding chairs, and coolers when they barbecue on the Fourth of July. Maybe his grandson will torment those two could-be twin girls and they will run to him for succor, but he would give them no satisfaction. He'd take his grandson's part and shoo them away, reminding those could-be twins that boys will be boys.

When Leslie poked the turkey with a fork, the juices ran bloody.

It was too much for a man to have to do. He turned the oven off on the underdone bird. He would not wait for them to come. He sat at his dining room table, stiff and upright like a guest. He ate his side dishes straight from the pots. He ate methodically, taking small bites to make the meal last. Leslie Singleton ate with unwavering vigilance, for, if he relaxed, he'd soon move to the couch in front of the TV.

DISTURBANCE

WHEN SOPHIE ENTERED the house and dropped her outer things in the vestibule, the smell of smoke was faint, but present, as if a candle had burned down to the wick and now smoldered somewhere. "Mother!" she cried, racing through the living room for the kitchen, where the smell seemed strongest.

"In here dear."

Mrs. Newcomb was seated at the kitchen table, drinking coffee and Sophie's mother stood before the stove, skewering a piece of paper. The page was stuck through with one of the little sticks her mother kept for making kebobs. The flames licked at the page. It curled and blackened, a paper marshmallow.

"What are you doing?" Sophie asked.

Her mother waved the disintegrating page. "Oh, it's just a flyer," she said. "They're collecting signatures, asking us to pull you out of your Mr. Everett's class."

"Why?" Sophie asked.

Her mother turned her attention back to the stove and blithely continued to roast the paper.

"To show solidarity, dear," Mrs. Newcomb answered. "They want to present a united front. They're calling it *Keep Togetherness Together!* I'm going to go home and burn mine too."

"Good for you, Sadie." Her mother turned off the burner. She touched the blackened end of the skewer before tossing it into the sink. It fell apart at its tip and her finger was left smudged with ash. "How many today, Sophie?"

"Nine," she answered. "Including me." For the past two weeks the number of her classmates had dwindled, fewer and fewer showing up each day. Each day more and more parents were choosing to keep their children at home rather than have them remain under Mr. Everett's tutelage.

Mrs. Newcomb set her coffee mug down and rose from the table. "My Seth will be in class tomorrow," she said, eyeing Sophie appraisingly. "Just like it was any other day."

Sophie fidgeted under the buxom woman's gaze. Mrs. Newcomb always looked at her this way now. Her son Seth had been chosen for Sophie, but the two were many years away from being joined.

"So will my Sophie," her mother said. "She understands that this is not just about Mr. Everett. It's bigger than that. Sometimes you've got to take a stand. Right, Sophie?"

"Right," Sophie said—though really—she had no idea.

The next morning, there were only seven students in attendance. They sat, enshrouded in semi-darkness, waiting to see what their teacher would do next. Mr. Everett stood before them, wavering, his shadow seeming to melt. Sophie could barely see him through the darkness. Five minutes before, she and the others had been sitting at their desks and learning about waves. Mr. Everett had dropped a pebble into the glass tank of water on his desk and the class had watched as the pebble caused a series of tiny waves. He had told them that the waves were caused by the surface of the water being subjected to disturbance and then he'd zoned out right in front of them. He'd stood there for a time, as if frozen to the spot between desk and chalkboard and then—without warning—he'd jogged to the light switch by the door and turned out all of the lights. Now

Sophie and her classmates sat in the dark, pretending to be brave in the face of their teacher's unpredictable behavior.

Everything familiar became disorienting in the dark. Sophie could not see the town's flag standing tall in the corner between chalkboard and window. Normally, she could take comfort in its presence, in its unique pattern of orange, green, and purple—it was made using only secondary colors—but in the dark, she was without comfort. She didn't know how the rest of the class was faring. The other kids were scattered around the room, lost to her in a sea of darkness. In keeping with her pledge, Mrs. Newcomb had sent Seth to school that day. He'd been sitting in his usual spot at the desk to the right of Sophie's that morning, but Sophie had asked him to move, believing that if they all sat spread out it would make the classroom appear more full. It had been her way of doing her part. Now that she sat trembling in the dark for long lonely minutes, wishing Seth was seated beside her, she regretted her ingenuity.

If her mother were here she would fear neither the darkness nor Mr. Everett. Her mother would snap the teacher out of it. "Be nice to him," her mother had said that morning before sending Sophie off to school. "Remember he needs your support, not your fear."

Sophie pushed her seat back, gathering courage from the sound of the metal legs scraping across the floor. If she looked hard enough, she could make out silhouettes in the dark. Like the big one near where she thought the classroom door should be. Surely that one was Mr. Everett, slumped near the light switch. Even from where she stood, Sophie could make out the drooping of his shoulders and the hang of his head. She made her way slowly, touching everything along the way—sometimes the edge of a desk, sometimes a shoulder or the top of a head—until she was at the front of the classroom and Mr. Everett was in her reach. He was whispering something. It sounded like "Julie, God help me." Sophie couldn't remember if Julie was his wife or his daughter. She wasn't supposed to know what had caused Mr. Everett's new and erratic behavior, but like all of the other children who kept silent in the presence of adults, she drank everything in. All of her classmates knew that Mr. Everett's wife had left him, taking their daughter with her. Though Sophie knew this, neither she nor her classmates nor anyone else in the town of Togetherness knew what had prompted Mrs. Everett's drastic measure. Strangely comforted by his whispering, Sophie made her way more securely through the dark. She wondered if he'd been whispering the entire time she'd been approaching. If she'd remained in her seat, she'd never have heard him. Standing there in the dark beside Mr. Everett had a soothing effect upon Sophie. His whisper was a private thing between the two of them, something meant only for her ears. Knowing her mother would want it this way, Sophie grasped in the darkness and took hold of the teacher's hand. Keeping her voice whisper soft, she asked, "Won't you come home with me for dinner?"

Seated at the head of the dinner table, Mr. Everett ate everything Sophie's mother placed before him and complimented the meal profusely. Sophie didn't tell her mother what happened earlier that day, but she watched Mr. Everett closely, waiting to see if the teacher would do or say something peculiar. The teacher seemed normal enough, even happy to have been invited, though there were several times when he looked at Sophie as if he were about to speak, his mouth opening and closing like a fish's, without emitting any sound.

To Sophie's mother he complained, "Everyone treats me like a leper. No one will come near me."

"We're not like that," her mother assured him.

"There are so few left in my class now. I've barely got a handful."

"That just means Sophie can have more individual attention," her mother said.

He thanked her mother for allowing Sophie to remain in his class. "They're waging a war against me, you know. They're trying to shut me down," he said. "No one trusts me anymore."

Her mother looked at her and tapped the table twice, a signal for Sophie to clear the dishes. Once Sophie got up and removed the plates, her mother turned her chair at an angle, crossed her legs and opened a pack of cigarettes. Smoking, she said, "If we're not careful, we'll soon be like the folks *on the outside.*"

Sophie perked up at this. Rarely did her mother ever mention the outside world, a place from which the townsfolk had fought to separate themselves, a place Sophie scarcely thought of. Like any other educable child in Togetherness, Sophie knew the story of the town's founding as well as she knew her prayers. Twenty years ago—ten years before she was born—one hundred families of like-minded interests and values had gathered together and decided to leave the outside world behind. Grieved and appalled by the way most of the people they'd encountered kept to themselves, coming together only for selfish and temporary reasons, the one hundred families had pooled their resources to obtain a land grant, a charter and a ninety-nine year lease to forge an existence far away from the rest of the world. Rebelling against what they saw as a depraved way of life, the one hundred families fled it, striking out on their own, seeking not to tell the rest of the world how to live, but only to free themselves from the rest of the world. Like those who called upon the dictates of their religious faith to recuse themselves from military service or jury duty, the one hundred founder families had looked to the dictates of their spirits and recused themselves from the world. They had not seceded so much as they had claimed moral asylum. Collectively, they remitted their taxes to the government for the right to be left alone and govern themselves according to their own best interests. Seeking only a peaceful existence, wanting merely to be left alone to live as best they saw fit, they'd built the town from scratch. Upon the acres of land they'd purchased, they'd built not only homes and industries, but a way of life. They'd planted their values and beliefs into the soil and up had sprung Togetherness, a town where relationships were not only celebrated and valued, but were a requirement for citizenship.

From where Sophie stood, there was no indication that the outside world truly existed. For all she knew, Togetherness was the only town in the world. There were no visitors, no strangers, no nothing to indicate that anything on the outside mattered. But her father had died defending the town from *on the outsiders*, so maybe that was all the proof she needed. And now too, there was Mrs. Everett who had slipped away and into that world of which Sophie knew so little. "Is it really as bad as everyone says?" Sophie asked.

Mr. Everett and her mother shared a look just then and the conversation took a turn. They began to talk about different people in town, swapping stories and gossip like old friends. Neither of them mentioned the world on the outside or "the incident" that was responsible for Mr. Everett's current fall from grace. But Sophie knew as much about it as everyone else; their enclave of a town was too small to harbor secrets. A man without a family, a man who had been deserted, abandoned, left by his spouse, Mr. Everett was now an anomaly in their small relationship-driven town. Only adult couples who had been joined to partners for a minimum of eight years could live permanently in Togetherness. The couples signed contracts giving their pledges to remain joined together and to have their children joined to others immediately upon adulthood. Now that Mr. Everett was unjoined, the townsfolk worried that keeping him in the classroom would improperly influence the children who were his students and cause a wave of immoral behavior. The members of the town could proudly boast that there had been no divorces since the town's chartering and inception twenty years ago. But, now, thanks to Mr. Everett, there was a separation on the town's books, "the incident" as it was now being called. Nothing like Mr. Everett had ever happened before.

Dinner over, Mr. Everett rose from the table and bowed deep from the waist like a gallant. "I really appreciate this," he said. "Really, I do." He looked down at Sophie as he said it and she knew then that she had been right to keep the secret from early in the day, right not to tell her mother what Mr. Everett had done.

"You're more than welcome to eat with us any night. Come again tomorrow," her mother said. "Unless you prefer to be alone."

"No one prefers that," he said.

Her mother walked Mr. Everett to the door and helped him into his coat. He shrugged into it and turned to face her. Holding her mother's arms lightly, he then leaned in to kiss her. It was a perfect solution, Sophie thought. Neither of them had anybody anymore. It would be a sensible pairing. But Sophie doubted it would ever happen with her dead father standing in the way. Though her mother had been alone for some time, she'd never ceased to speak of Sophie's father or let the memory of him fade.

Once released, her mother went to the door and held it open for Mr. Everett. There was neither passion nor interest in her eyes when she told the teacher, "I wish you hadn't done that."

Mr. Everett never came home directly with Sophie after the first night. He always arrived some two hours afterwards looking freshly showered and changed. When asked about it, Sophie's mother said it was better this way, not only because it gave Mr. Everett something to look forward to while he decompressed from the day, but also because it gave them a chance to prepare for his coming. Sophie didn't know what needed preparing, but each day before Mr. Everett's visit, her mother found some small task for her.

On the fourth night her mother said, "Here Sophie, come help me tidy up." She beckoned Sophie into the living room and set her to plumping the sofa pillows.

After taking a pillow from the couch and punching it in its middle as she'd been taught, Sophie asked, "How come we're on Mr. Everett's side?" The question had been burning in her ever since the first students started disappearing and her mother had declared that she would not allow Sophie to be one of them. Sophie was glad that her mother wasn't boycotting Mr. Everett, but she didn't understand why she was taking such a staunch stand against the rest of the townspeople.

"To show solidarity," her mother said.

"But the other day Mrs. Newcomb said that the petition was for solidarity."

"That's one version of it," her mother said. She took a small hand vacuum and buzzed it along the cushions. "Mr. Everett is one of the original members of this town and we owe him our reverence and respect. Showing solidarity with him is a way of upholding the principles we believe in Sophie, principles that your father died fighting for."

Though Togetherness was a firmly established and legally recognized town, its dwellers received occasional challenges from outsiders and Sophie's father had died in a skirmish four years ago defending their town and its way of life. She understood now why her mother was so adamant. Somehow, this thing with Mr. Everett was all about Sophie's dead father, though Sophie couldn't see how it was. She hung her head. In the excitement of the past few weeks, she'd forgotten her father's memory. She was supposed to say a prayer for him every night, but she had recently let many nights go by wherein she did not.

"Pray, Sophie that you never end up alone and have to go through what Mr. Everett is going through." Sophie thought her mother meant the ostracizing, but the look in her eyes said she meant something else entirely. "Trust me, you wouldn't want to know the feeling."

When Sophie still said nothing, her mother grew impatient. She set the hand vacuum down in the middle of the seat cushion and crossed her arms in front of her. "You do like Mr. Everett don't you?"

Sophie thought back to the very first day of class. After introducing himself and making everyone go round with an icebreaker, Mr. Everett had promised that he would never raise his voice to any student, never force anyone to stand and recite, never use the ruler or the paddle and never make anyone stand in the corner. And he hadn't. He had kept his word. Yes, Sophie liked him immensely. "He's pretty nice," she said.

The bell rang.

"Good," her mother said. "Because he's here."

But it wasn't Mr. Everett at the door after all. It was Mrs. Newcomb. She bustled in and peered around. "Where is he?"

"Not yet Sadie," Sophie's mother said.

"Well, how am I going to show the fellow my support if he doesn't even show up?"

"He will," Sophie's mother soothed. "You're early."

Once Mr. Everett arrived, the adults sat down to the table that Sophie had helped to set. Dinner was a quiet affair, devoid of the usual desultory conversation Sophie had come to expect from her teacher. The appearance of Mrs. Newcomb at the dinner table seemed to render Mr. Everett shy. Mrs. Newcomb watched Mr. Everett alertly, as if waiting for him to speak, but the teacher kept his eyes on his plate, unconscious of her scrutiny. The meal ran its course in silence. Oblivious to the reticence of the adults, Sophie ate with the heartiness of a hungry young girl.

After dinner, her mother led their guests to the living room while Sophie prepared the drinks.

"Have a seat," Sophie's mother said. "Make yourself comfortable."

Mrs. Newcomb seated herself immediately and patted the seat on the couch beside her for Mr. Everett to join her.

Sophie brought in coffee and tea. As soon as she set the drinks on the table, the three adults reached for them. Though Mrs. Newcomb and her mother had taken coffee, Sophie noticed that Mr. Everett took tea. Sophie took a cup of tea for herself as well.

"Have you heard anything since?" Mrs. Newcomb asked. It had been almost three weeks since Mrs. Everett had disappeared.

The teacher's eyes watered. "No," Mr. Everett said, blowing the word into the cup. Sophie watched it whispering it across the surface of his hot tea, disturbing the calm of the piping hot water and the calm of the adults seated on either side of him.

Before Mrs. Newcomb could follow up, Sophie's mother sent her a quelling look. "Perhaps we should talk of more delightful things."

"Of course," Mrs. Newcomb said, duly chastised. She looked at Sophie and brightened. "My Seth is at home completing his science homework. Seth says he's learning so much in class now." With every word spoken, Mrs. Newcomb's voice rose higher. "Most likely, it's because he's getting so much more personalized attention now." Mrs. Newcomb sat back against the seat cushions and gave Sophie and her mother an exaggerated conspiratorial wink.

"Sophie, is your homework all done?" her mother asked.

"Yes," Sophie said. She'd completed her homework during the day. Mr. Everett had recently instituted a new thing called "Reflection Time" where no talking was allowed. Instead, everyone was to sit quietly and make no disturbing noises. Sophie's best girlfriend Kristen had not shown up for the past two days, and since Sophie had no one with whom she could pass notes, she used Reflection Time to complete the homework that she knew Mr. Everett would never grade. During Reflection Time, Mr. Everett sat at his desk with the previous day's homework in front of him, looking down at the slim stack without seeming to really see it. They were still on waves and just that day Sophie had learned about the great and destructive tsunami wave. But there had been no demonstration like before. Though the earth science lessons still continued, Mr. Everett no longer used props to make the learning come alive. The surface of the water in the tank on his desk remained calm and undisturbed.

Mr. Everett looked up from his tea with troubled eyes. He said, "I fear for her. She's out there somewhere and she's got my little girl with her."

"What's out there?" Sophie asked.

"You wouldn't want to know," he said. The hands which held the cup trembled.

"I would," Sophie insisted.

"It's horrible! So horrible. What a world! No satisfaction. No contentment. Children didn't want to grow up to be anything other than famous. No one spoke to anyone. People spent all of their time playing with little gadgets. We lost our sense of each other, of why we were here in the first place. There was no common good, nothing to work for, to strive for. Nothing to protect or preserve. It was just an empty world. We were all becoming hollow."

"You mean shallow?" Sophie asked.

"Hollow," he said. "I know what I mean. You could change anything out there. If you didn't like something about yourself, you could just replace it. You don't like your face? You could go and get a new face. New hair. New eye color. New anything. Empty on the inside. Hollow. We all originally came together because the world outside had degenerated from a tolerable place into a terrible place. Men were walking into movie theatres and opening fire on moviegoers, killing and wounding dozens upon dozens of people at a time. Children were being placed in washing machines for kicks. Teenage boys were beaten and killed for wearing the hoods of their sweatshirts pulled over their head. And even when there was no physical violence, there was still all of the visual violence."

Sophie was losing the thread of the conversation. "Visual violence?"

Mrs. Newcomb explained, "It assaulted the eyes. It was everywhere you turned. Little girls like you couldn't turn on a television or open a magazine without being assaulted by images that told them their only value in this world was sexual."

Mr. Everett said, "The people around us were mindless like zombies. So many of them were addicted to harmful substances. One man even attacked another man and chewed off a portion of his face."

"I remember that," her mother said. "It makes sense with all of this evil surrounding you that you would want to leave it all behind."

"But Julie didn't want to come," he said. "She said we all were separatists. She thought that we were actually making the problem worse by removing ourselves from the equation. She said we were taking some of the few people who actually could see through the muck and mire and removing them rather than using them to help."

"Help? Help what?" Mrs. Newcomb asked.

Mr. Everett mumbled something that no one could understand. Sophie's mother asked him to repeat himself.

"Help make the world a better place," he said. His embarrassment was clear.

Her mother looked startled. "What a quaint idea," she said, reaching for a cigarette and indulging in a habit Sophie didn't remember her ever having back when her father was still alive. "It's been a long time since I've heard such a sentiment."

Mr. Everett leaned forward and eyed her mother. "Do you miss it?"

Sophie also edged closer, curious to hear what her mother would say. Leaving the cigarette behind, her mother rose from her seat and walked over to the wide window which looked out onto their front lawn. She tugged at the gossamer curtain as if she would yank it from its rod, then she trailed her fingers down the thin yellow silk. "I do my fair share of complaining about the small-mindedness of some of the folks here in the community, about the pettiness I've encountered since becoming a widow. Perhaps it's my way of lashing out, getting some small and fine revenge because of the way they've treated me since I lost my husband." Her mother let go of the curtain and wrapped her arms around herself. "But at the end of the day, if this is all that I have to complain about, coldness on the part of a handful of people who don't know what to do with difference, then I'd say I'm far better off. I remember that world out there. I can't quite ever get it out of my head. For the first years of living here I still heard gunshots where there weren't ever any gunshots. I couldn't stop looking over my shoulder whenever I walked home at night or pulled into my garage. Once

Sophie was born I finally realized that none of those dangers were here and I finally stopped hearing the gunshots. Do I miss it? Always wondering about my safety? Knowing there was no sense, no rhyme or reason to the way certain people behaved? There's nothing out there for me to miss."

"Certainly not," Mrs. Newcomb agreed. "What a world it was!" She reached for a magazine and began to fan herself with it. "That world was just a place of falseness. False people. False apologies and false forgiveness. Sophie, anyone could subject anybody else to any sort of cruelty—betrayal, physical abuse, neglect, insincerity and just plain meanness—and it was all to be forgiven so long as the person eventually apologized. And of course, the apology wasn't the kind to be trusted. It was a one size fits all kind of apology. All the people who had caused so much suffering, hurt and pain had to do was say something like 'I meant no harm. I'm sorry for anything and everything I've ever done to hurt you.'"

"Then what?" Sophie asked.

Mrs. Newcomb shrugged. "Then you were supposed to forgive them."

"Just like that?" she asked.

This time her mother answered. "Just like that."

Even she, a girl too young to be joined, could see the clear wrong of such a practice, the falseness of the blanket apology, the ease of the absolution. Sophie had been taught that there could be no sincere apology without acknowledgment, repentance and atonement. Any other apology was purely a performance, as insincere as a thief apologizing for shoplifting while refusing to return the stolen items.

"There's more," Mr. Everett said. "If you were wronged and didn't immediately forgive the other person, then the blame shifted from him or her to you simply because you wouldn't get over it!"

Sophie was glad that she had never known that outside world of which the three adults had spoken. As she listened to them speak disparagingly of the world they'd left behind, it became clear to her that she stood apart from them. It wasn't just that they were older. It was something else entirely, something she'd never noticed, never even thought of until that moment. There was a time when all three of them had been outsiders, something that she had never been and would never be. Sophie had lived in Togetherness her whole life. She'd been born in the town, born to the town. She didn't know anything else, she did not have stories of the outside world, she didn't know of any other life outside of this one. She had lived her entire life in this town that these three adults had helped to build. The three people sitting across from her had all come from elsewhere. They'd lived other lives, seen other things, had been a part of the outside world. They had stories between them which they could share or withhold, stories which Sophie herself could never fathom. Whatever they might tell her would be as alien to her understanding of the world and its workings as the story of a space creature who'd beamed down to describe life on his home planet.

"It sounds awful," Sophie said.

"I don't think Julie saw it that way," Mr. Everett said. "She saw the hope and the possibility when all I saw was danger and despair. I just wanted to keep her safe and I could never do that out there in the world."

"No, you never could have," Sophie's mother said.

After Mrs. Newcomb left, Sophie's mother and Mr. Everett continued to talk quietly. Sophie emptied her mother's ashtray and replenished the teacher's tea and still the two adults kept talking. By the time Mrs. Newcomb left, Sophie understood that the evening had been part of her mother's plan. Mrs. Newcomb had been invited not only to make Mr. Everett feel that he had more support than that of which he was aware, but also so that Mrs. Newcomb might take his story to the other parents and report back. Sophie's mother could not have done it;

she was a widow and no one would have listened or taken her word for anything. But Mrs. Newcomb—strong, stalwart and Seth-doting— could be sent as an emissary to sway Mr. Everett's detractors.

The second time Sophie came to refresh his tea, Mr. Everett was lamenting over his dwindling number of students. Since the incident with the lights, three more kids had been pulled out of his class. Now there were only four attending. He told Sophie's mother that *Keep Togetherness Together!* signs had been posted on his house and that threatening messages had been written on his car.

As Sophie leaned over to pour out the hot water, she heard Mr. Everett say, "Taking my students was clearly just the first step. From here on out, it's only going to get worse."

And it did.

The next week when Sophie attempted to enter the schoolhouse, she was prevented from doing so by parents standing arm-in-arm, blocking the entrance. She returned home early to find her mother kneeling on the lawn. When Sophie came nearer she saw that her mother was gathering small paper-covered rocks and making piles of them on the grass. "What are you doing?"

"These are the ones that missed," her mother said.

She followed her mother's gaze. The lower windows of their house had been egged. Several windows had been broken.

When she faced her mother again, she saw her peeling one of the papers from a rock. "What does it say?" she asked.

Her mother refused to show Sophie the words.

"Because of Mr. Everett?"

The phone rang and her mother ran inside to answer it. Sophie followed her into the house, but went into a different room and silently picked up the other receiver. She heard a stranger's voice. The voice shouted at her mother, saying too many things too loudly and angrily for Sophie to understand. Sophie recoiled from the anger and the volume. Without waiting to see how her mother might respond, she slipped the phone back into its cradle.

After the letter-covered rocks, there were thinly veiled discussions on the radio stations. There were *Keep Togetherness Together!* pamphlets and flyers. Then there were the bumper stickers. And the large white wooden signs stuck deep into the ground in front of their house that were just like the ones on Mr. Everett's lawn.

Then there were the people. They waited outside in packs, hoping for a glimpse of Sophie or her mother. Her mother predicted that they would soon get bored and go away. Instead they stayed. Each day their numbers increased as more and more came. Sophie didn't even realize there were so many people in her town. It was as if the whole town was there at once, outside on their lawn. They were angry at her and her mother but Sophie didn't know why. When asked, her mother adopted the same tone she'd used to explain the birds and the bees. She explained that sometimes living in a place like Togetherness could be difficult, but that Sophie shouldn't blame the folks in town. Her mother said that they didn't know any better and were just suspicious of other people's ways. The only problem was that Sophie, her mother and Mr. Everett were now the other people. Sophie pretended to accept the simplified explanation, but she thought to herself that there must surely have been some townsfolk who supported Mr. Everett. Surely, there had to be some people that were on their side, but who they might be, Sophie couldn't guess.

One week later, Sophie woke up to find the crowd had dispersed. She came out from her bedroom and went down the stairs and opened the front door to find the protesters gone. Only their debris remained. She went outside and stood on the dew-covered lawn and slowly began to pick up their trash. The townsfolk had left their wrappings, their cups and their straws. Every now and then, Sophie picked up a crumpled dollar and pocketed it. Soon her mother came out and joined her. Stunned, neither of them mentioned the absence of the crowd.

Sophie was the first to see Mr. Everett approaching from across the street. She waved, although she felt much more like mourning. Mr. Everett looked like a broken man. His clothing was disheveled, his hair uncombed and his eyes bleary. He looked to her as if he hadn't slept in some time. Sophie had never seen him like this before. She didn't know what to say to him when he crossed onto their lawn.

"Rough night?" her mother asked, scooping trash into a large plastic bag.

Mr. Everett kicked at an empty can of soda and sent it clanging down the pavement. "I don't have anything left," he said. "Nothing at all. They took it. Everything."

Sophie thought the teacher had been robbed. She dropped her trash back onto the lawn and approached him, intending to take his hand the way she had done that first day in the classroom when he'd turned off the lights. She reached for his hand and Mr. Everett grabbed her and turned her, holding her in front of him, his forearm crushing her neck. Her mother screamed. Mr. Everett backed away from her mother, dragging Sophie with him.

"They burned my house down," he said.

"I'm sorry," Sophie choked out, assuming that he was talking to her. It was only right that he should blame her. After all, she had taken him from the classroom that day and brought him home. Maybe none of it would have happened if she hadn't.

"Sophie, don't move!" her mother cried.

Pressed against him as she was, Sophie couldn't have moved if she'd wanted to. She smelled the acrid scent of smoke on his clothing and wondered how long Mr. Everett had fought with the fire. He smelled like something burning. A fierce calm took Sophie. She wasn't scared at all. Although the face of his watch bit into her throat, she didn't think Mr. Everett would ever really hurt her.

"Let her go!" It was her mother's voice again, but Sophie barely recognized it. Already she was distancing herself from it all, already she was slipping away, regarding her mother as a woman she faintly knew, already she was siding with Mr. Everett.

"I can't," he said. "They'll never let me go. It's the only way."

Her mother's face was fierce and sharp. "So you'll hurt us? We've been kind to you."

He shook his head. "No, not you. Her, maybe. She's been kind. You think I can't see your pity for what it is? I don't need your help or your dinners."

"I don't want you to take my daughter out there," her mother said. "Julie's out there. My daughter's out there!"

"Please don't hurt my baby," Sophie's mother cried. "Don't take her hostage."

Sophie listened as if this all were happening to someone else. She was not terribly interested in the outcome. She and Mr. Everett would go. That she knew. Her mother would not be able to stop the two of them. They were tsunami waves, big and seeking, moved by forces of nature beyond their control. Her mother could not hold them back.

Mr. Everett said, "It's a kindness, really. She doesn't belong here. She'll see everything differently once we're gone."

Mr. Everett, don't be scared. I'll go away with you, Sophie wanted to say.

"You won't hurt her?" Her mother was crying now, the sharpness gone.

"I—would—never—hurt—" He looked at his arm and seemed surprised to find her throat crushed behind it.

"Take me with you," her mother said. "I don't belong here either anymore."

"No. I don't think so?" There was a question in his voice, as if her mother had the answer.

Her mother pressed on. "We'll look like a family traveling all together."

"A family?" Mr. Everett asked as if he'd never heard those words put together in just that way. "Traveling? Together?"

"Yes," her mother said, nodding and smiling as though to a child.

"A family," he whispered. Sophie felt his arm slacken at her throat.

"Come Sophie," her mother said, holding out her hand. Mr. Everett let her go.

"Go and get your things," he said, following close behind. "Hurry!"

Her mother led her up the stairs to her bedroom. It seemed to Sophie as if she'd been away from the room for days and years rather than minutes. Her mother lingered at the window in Sophie's bedroom and Sophie looked around the strange room, knowing that it was hers but not really believing it. Ever since Mr. Everett said she was going with him, it had not been hers.

Sophie sat on the bed while her mother packed for her. It did not seem real to her that this thing could be so easily done, their lives wrapped and tidied so neatly, but there was the proof of it in her mother's slow but efficient packing. Her head bent over an opened suitcase, her mother said, "If there's something you want to keep, you'd better take it now, Sophie." Sophie felt no sentimental attachment to any of the items her mother packed; she had a feeling that she wouldn't need these things in her new life. Mr. Everett hovered in the doorway like a specter, oddly silent and watchful. Sophie sat back against the bed, ignoring her mother's urgings. Briefly, she wondered if Seth would miss her if she went away with Mr. Everett or if he would begin to keep company with Kristen, the Newcomb's second choice for him. She'd always liked knowing that Kristen was runner-up to her, second in all the ways that counted, but now as she thought of Mr. Everett waiting just outside her bedroom door, standing at the edge of the stair's landing, Seth did not seem like such a concern. Kristen could have him. Sophie was putting away her childish things now. She liked Seth well enough, but now she saw that Seth meant nothing and never could.

As soon as they left the house, the crowd converged upon them. Signaled by Sophie's mother at the window, the townspeople came and blocked the pathway between the front door and the car, surrounding them on all sides, separating Sophie's mother from Mr. Everett and trying to separate Sophie too. Sophie was holding Mr. Everett's hand tightly, too scared to look up and see how he was taking all of this. The parents, the townspeople, were all so many tall bodies surrounding her that she saw only torsos, buttons and belts. She gave Mr. Everett's hand a squeeze to let him know that she would follow, that they would stay together no matter what, but Mr. Everett did not squeeze back. He looked down at her and spoke to her one last time, in as gentle a voice as the one he'd used that fateful day she'd overheard him in class. Then he let go of Sophie's hand and allowed the crowd to devour him. So loud was it in its satisfaction to have him it did not stop to hear his last words. Sophie was the only one close enough to hear. Later, when her mother asked her, she would pretend not to know. She would keep the secret and never tell anyone that in the end Mr. Everett had apologized. He'd said that he hadn't meant to disturb anyone. He'd apologized for any harm he might have caused. He had said that he was sorry—so sorry—for everything.

MOST HONEST

MY WIFE'S VOICE comes across the receiver, plaintive and unforget-table. "I need a favor. Can you take Marissa tonight?"

"Good morning," I say. Divorce or not, I am still worth the com-mon courtesy of a greeting.

"Sorry," she says. "So…can you? I'd really appreciate it."

We are no longer married, and that is why we talk like this. My wife does not indulge in idle chatter. When she calls, there is always a rea-son, always an explanation. Me, I never have to explain. I never call.

She says, "I know it's not the weekend, but I wouldn't ask if it weren't important."

"Who's the lucky guy?"

"I don't think you should ask that sort of thing."

"Should I pick her up from school?"

"If you get her around six, it's fine."

"Must be a dinner date," I say. One annoyed breath later she hangs up.

Conversations with my wife are among the things that I don't miss. Had she not called, I'd still be asleep. That's another thing I don't miss. Waking up early because she has to get up at five and have lights and music in the morning.

Every morning now, I wake up reminded that I am newly single and that it is a good thing. I always wake up on the side of the bed farthest from the door, the side that used to be hers. Having to sleep on the lumpy side is another thing I do not miss.

I start each day enjoying my new small freedoms. I keep a list of them on the refrigerator where I can be sure to see it each morning as I take out the milk for my cereal for the breakfast I eat in a kitchen free of the clutter of useless appliances for extravagant dishes that no one but an accredited chef actually knows how to make. (I do not miss the garlic press).

It seems like I should have a say in this, like she should need my permission to go on this date.

Once a week, I add a new freedom to my list, but today I can't think of anything to add because I am looking at the list and thinking of this date and pouring milk over my cereal and missing my wife and now the bowl is filled with milk and my cereal floats in the milk and milk is now spilling over the bowl and down onto my bare feet and I'm still looking at the list and missing her hard, so hard.

Now I have to knock on my own front door. No use trying my old key. My daughter comes out bundled, dragging a bag seemingly meant for an extended stay. Marissa watches me uncertainly, then drops her bag and runs to me.

"Hi, Pumpkin," I say, all of my life in the words.

I've never picked her up from home before. My wife always drops her off at an innocuous location. (McDonald's.) That way, I have no excuse to drop by my house which is no longer where I live. That she is allowing me to pick up Marissa here means something. Maybe the guy is such a loser she doesn't want Marissa to meet him. Or maybe she's so eager to get to him she doesn't want to waste time with a drop-off.

Marissa pulls off her hat and asks, "Daddy, do you like it?"

My daughter's hair lies smooth against her scalp. Parted down the middle, her hair is gathered at either side of her head and pulled up high and then braided, secured at the tops by brightly colored bobbles resembling gumballs and at the bottoms by plastic barrettes in the shape of butterflies. Always before—when we lived as a family—my wife had braided Marissa's hair into elaborate and pain-staking patterns which her hair would hold for weeks at a time until the braids grew too fuzzy to ignore and had to be redone. I'd watch the two of them seated in the living room, my wife on the sofa and Marissa on the floor between my wife's knees, her head leaning back as her mother fashioned her a surprise hairstyle. Now my wife takes Marissa to the salon and has them put a relaxer in her hair. This is to make things more manageable, to free my wife up from one more task now that she is a busy single mother with much too much to do.

"I like it." I smooth down Marissa's already smooth hair and hug her to me.

I need these minutes with my daughter, hugging her, to brace myself. When I finally look at my wife, her appearance comes as a surprise. She'd stopped wearing makeup because I'd once complained about all the smudges left on my clothing and the expense of the dry cleaning bills. Now, here she is, lipsticked and powdered, her brows tamed into thin, arched lines. She's poised and grim, as if meeting me at our house is a battle she's had to train for.

"You look nice," I say, unable to help it. Too late do I recall her disdain of the mediocre compliment. "If 'nice' is the best you can do when I'm all dressed up, I'd rather you just didn't say anything," she'd once told me, pointing out that I gave her the same compliment when she was dressed in jeans or sweats.

"Thanks," my wife says, making a moue of displeasure. Apparently, she remembers that talk, too.

Marissa says, "Oh Daddy, I forgot Munchkin." Dropping my hand, she runs back into the house for the stuffed elf I'd won for her at Coney Island when she was three. Holding Marissa's bag, my wife guards the door, blocking it. According to my wife, Marissa began sleeping with this elf again soon after The Divorce. (Divorce is my wife's word. I prefer *dissolution*. It makes our marriage sound like a crystalline substance, glittery yet hard, succumbing to forces greater than itself.) Now she refuses to sleep without it. According to my wife, Marissa clings to the thing all night, holding tightly, needing it.

Marissa gets into my car and pulls on her seatbelt. "Daddy, can I get a milkshake instead of a soda with my Happy Meal this time?" she asks. "I want strawberry, okay?"

"Pumpkin, we're not going to McDonald's tonight. We're going home."

She climbs up onto her knees to look out the passenger's window at the house, then turns back to me and says, "But we are."

The outing with my daughter, if it can be called such, doesn't go well. I usually have grand plans, but today was a surprise and I'm strapped for cash. I've never brought her back to my apartment until now. The disappointment starts before Marissa even sees the place, once I tell her that her bedroom and the living room are one and the same. When we go inside, she takes one look at the apartment's ransacked appearance, at my socks curled in a hallway corner with my underwear and soiled tee shirts, at the puddle of milk pooled in front of the refrigerator and says, "I want to go home. Now."

Back at our house there is only one light on in the living room; its dim yellow haze shows through where the blinds stop short. I know the lamp, an ugly little thing my wife inherited from her college roommate. My wife and her date are probably seated next to each other on the couch near the ugly little lamp with the stereo behind them tuned to something mellow and commercial free. They have likely come to the part of the evening where people say the clever yet noncommittal things that increase the likelihood of sex.

I ring the bell.

I didn't mean to come here. After two hours of the cartoon chan-nel, I gave Marissa a bath and put her to bed. Now here I am. I didn't mean to leave my daughter alone and asleep back in my apartment. I only meant to shower after dinner and settle in for the night, but when I stepped out of the shower, I'd felt the way I had when we were dating in college and my only thoughts were of seeing her. I didn't mean to come here. I am no longer in college on my way to pick up my girl. And she is no longer my girl. We share only the merging of our genetic makeup and even then we merely take turns.

My wife opens the door. "What are you doing here?"

"Can I come in?" I step into my old house. There is no one else in the living room with my wife. Her shoes curl on their sides beneath the coffee table and a nearly empty glass of water sits beside a hard-backed book above the table. The stereo is off, its face silent and gleaming.

"Where's Marissa? Is everything okay?"

"She's fine," I say, taking a seat. "I put her to bed for the night. I just needed to drive around for a while."

"So you came *here*?"

"I didn't mean to." It is a strange feeling, sitting on my own couch in my own house with my own wife when neither one belongs to me. Her glass of water rests atop a hand carved coaster that resembles kitchen countertops. I lift the glass and hold the slippery, disc-like thing. "Is this new?"

"This isn't funny."

"So where's your date?"

"Is that why you're here? You came to meet—"

"—That's not why," I say.

"Well?"

"Sit down." I pull her down beside me.

"Okay, I'm sitting." She looks at me in a way she hasn't in a long time, like she's really listening, like she really wants to hear what I have to say. She has eased her shoulders back against the couch and her hands rest softly against her thighs. For the first time I can remember, I have her full attention. This is the closest we have been to each other in far too long. Two people on a couch, inches apart, not separated by the steel and metal of the car doors we use as barriers. I am taking a picture of her as she is in this moment. I snap the shot in my mind where I hold all of my pictures of her since my wife kept the albums, and I lodge it in a far corner where I know it can't run amok and crush me like only a fresh memory of her can.

"The night I moved out, I got drunk," I tell her.

"You don't drink," she says.

I'd never been one for drinking, but before I'd even bought cookware or groceries for my new apartment, I'd bought alcohol—rum, vodka, whiskey and scotch (I have no preference, no signature drink. Drunk is drunk is drunk to me). My wife would never let us keep alcohol in the house, not even safely stashed away, for fear that Marissa would get into it and become a closet alcoholic. Moving in to a one-bedroom apartment that day, I'd finally realized that my wife would never be my wife again and I drank myself into a stupor. My inebriation made me fearless enough to call her. I called her over and over again until she eventually stopped answering the phone. Then I just lay on the couch, calling her name until I passed out. I awakened alone the following day feeling sore and smelling sour, with an imprint of the couch's cushion on my forehead.

"Is that what this about? You want a drink?" she asks, as if I am a stranger and she a hostess gracious enough to oblige.

"No, that's not it. I—"

"You're in a very strange mood."

What I want to say to her is, I want you. I want my old life. I want what we had even though you think it was terrible.

I reach for her hand. "You look beautiful. Really beautiful. Your date—"

"There wasn't any date," she says. "I just wanted some time alone."

"You could have told me. I would have still taken her."

She leaned down and slipped her shoes back on. "Talking to you isn't so easy."

I should have known better. Random and impetuous dating was not her thing. It had taken me three months of trying to get her to agree to go out with me. She'd wanted more from her life than to end up as her mother. Instead she'd gotten me.

"You can talk to me now," I say. "I'm listening. You can say whatever you like. Whatever you need."

"You don't mean that."

"Honest," I say. "You can talk to me." But I am looking at her and seeing the picture of her in my mind and realizing that I am inches away from my own wife in my own house and we are not mad at each other, not hating—not loving either—but not hating. We are not cutting each other's words off, not slamming doors, not walking away. We are not keeping our distance. We are here. We are home.

I kiss her.

My wife's lips know the man I am and the man that I could be if she didn't push push push. Now I am pushing, pushing through all of our layers of accusation and guilt and blame, pushing through layers of clothing to find my wife, to join her until we are no longer separated.

"I still love you," I say.

She pulls out of my arms. "Don't say that. Please…just don't, okay?"

"What's wrong now?" I brush a few strands of hair off her face. "We just made love."

"We had sex. We did *not* make love." My wife reaches for her clothing. She struggles into her top and smoothes down her skirt "We're divorced. I don't love you any more."

To her, it is that simple. You divorce someone, sign the paperwork that severs what God has joined, divide your assets and possessions less than equally and that is that. Affection, emotion, memories, all the byproducts of love become null and void. We are divorced, dissolved; therefore we no longer love. Yet I still do.

"It's not that easy," I say.

"Sometimes it is," she says.

"Even now, you could be pregnant," I say, although it is a dumb thing to say and I took Sex Ed like everyone else.

"No, I can't," she says.

"You're right. It's too soon to know."

"No, you don't understand," she says. "I can't."

Leaning up on her elbows, she tells me she aborted a child of ours two years ago (I hadn't even known we were pregnant) and shortly afterwards had her tubes tied. She didn't want me to father any more of her children. I don't believe her until she reminds me of a particularly rough patch, weeks of arguing to no end.

She says, "That's when I just knew I couldn't do it. Not with you and the way we were. You wouldn't talk to me. I kept trying to talk to you. I kept trying to talk. Remember when I told you I needed to talk to you and said that it was important?"

"I think so," I say, hedging. There had been many times she'd said something of the sort to me. She'd been unhappy before she left me. That much I remember. She'd wanted to talk and I'd evaded, believing as I always did that problems would blow over or take care of themselves.

"You promised we would talk. You promised."

I am willing to believe some, but not all of it is my own fault. I know she's made sacrifices for me, though I've never asked her to. Before she asked for the divorce, she'd trotted out a string of my infractions. Things I couldn't even remember saying or doing. Things that sounded like something I'd said but not meant. Events, fights, and conversations that had long slipped from my memory. Promises and guarantees and assurances unkept. Admittedly, I could have been a better husband, but I was not all bad. I did not deserve this.

"Why tell me now?"

"It just seemed the most honest thing to do," she says, so calm.

I reach for my clothing. This is not real, I think. My daughter is sleeping alone in my apartment and I am here and this is not real. My wife is calm so calm I want to kill her. Her naked back bespeaks vulnerability as I search for a soft spot between her shoulder blades, a pressure point at the base of her neck. All the parts of her body that I used to trace and kiss now suggest possible ways of extinction. I can squeeze. I can kill. I touch her shoulder blade with my fingertips, brush the ends of her hair, curl my fingers around her soft pliable neck. She looks at my hand, not bothering to remove it. Speaking over cool bare shoulders, she says only "You won't."

I slam my fist into the stereo to feel something other than this, and my fourth and fifth knuckles explode with pain against the sturdy metal of the display panel. My wife crawls to the stereo and runs her hands over its face, gingerly testing the stop, play, forward and rewind buttons, smoothing the stereo's face lovingly like a child's.

I head home, trying not to think of the last hour. Instead I think of Marissa and how terrible it was to leave her, feeling it deep in my stomach. As I drive, I keep my foot on the gas and imagine all sorts of atrocities that end up with my daughter dead or assaulted. My building has a security system and an intercom, yet I imagine pedophiles scaling the walls and climbing in through windows to get to my unprotected daughter.

Maybe she's had a bad dream. Maybe she is sitting in front of the window crying silently, trying to be brave. Maybe she needs me. Maybe there is something I can do.

Marissa is sound asleep, her face turned to the window, her hair mussed, her cheek pressed against Munchkin's. I sit on the edge of the pull-out couch and watch my daughter sleep, scared to lose her, too. I am scared that there will be other prices to pay for my negligence, only I just won't be able to see them, just as I couldn't have seen that I'd have to mean the things I'd said long ago on nights I couldn't remember just as I couldn't have seen the things I couldn't see until it was too late.

I lie down by my daughter's blanketed feet and fight to stay awake. From this moment on, I will be vigilant. I will keep watch over all that I can ever have.

ACKNOWLEDGMENTS

"Lost and Found" first appeared in *Prairie Schooner*

"As I Wander" first appeared in *Shenandoah*

"The Loss of All Lost Things" first appeared in *Agni*

"What's Best for You" first appeared in *Pleiades* as "Voice on the
    Machine"

"Resident Lover" first appeared in *Jabberwock Review*

"Directory Assistance" first appeared in *Southwest Review*

"Cicero Waiting" first appeared in *The North American Review*

"A Brief Pause" first appeared in *Antioch Review*

"What Matters Most" first appeared in *Shenandoah*

"A Cup of My Time" first appeared in *Tampa Review*

"Intersections" first appeared in *Notre Dame Review*

"Navigator of Culture" first appeared in *Crab Orchard Review*

"Been Meaning to Say" first appeared in *Southwest Review*

"Disturbance" first appeared in *The Laurel Review*

"Most Honest" first appeared in *The New Guard*

AMINA GAUTIER teaches in the Department of English at the University of Miami. She is a winner of the Flannery O'Connor Award for Short Fiction for her debut story collection *At-Risk* and a winner of the Prairie Schooner Book Prize in Fiction for her sophomore collection *Now We Will Be Happy*. Her work has appeared in numerous literary journals, including *Agni*, *Callaloo*, *Glimmer Train*, *Iowa Review*, *Kenyon Review*, *Prairie Schooner*, *Southern Review*, and *StoryQuarterly*.

ALSO FROM ELIXIR PRESS

POETRY

Circassian Girl by Michelle Mitchell-Foust

Imago Mundi by Michelle Mitchell-Foust

Distance From Birth by Tracy Philpot

Original White Animals by Tracy Philpot

Flow Blue by Sarah Kennedy

A Witch's Dictionary by Sarah Kennedy

The Gold Thread by Sarah Kennedy

Monster Zero by Jay Snodgrass

Drag by Duriel E. Harris

Running the Voodoo Down by Jim McGarrah

Assignation at Vanishing Point by Jane Satterfield

Her Familiars by Jane Satterfield

The Jewish Fake Book by Sima Rabinowitz

Recital by Samn Stockwell

Murder Ballads by Jake Adam York

Floating Girl (Angel of War) by Robert Randolph

Puritan Spectacle by Robert Strong

Keeping the Tigers Behind Us by Glenn J. Freeman

Bonneville by Jenny Mueller

Cities of Flesh and the Dead by Diann Blakely

The Halo Rule by Teresa Leo

Perpetual Care by Katie Cappello

The Raindrop's Gospel: The Trials of St. Jerome and St. Paula
by Maurya Simon

Prelude to Air from Water by Sandy Florian

Let Me Open You A Swan by Deborah Bogen

Cargo by Kristin Kelly

Spit by Esther Lee

Rag & Bone by Kathryn Nuernberger

Kingdom of Throat-stuck Luck by George Kalamaras

Mormon Boy by Seth Brady Tucker

Nostalgia for the Criminal Past by Kathleen Winter

Little Oblivion by Susan Allspaw

Quelled Communiqués by Chloë Joan López

Stupor by David Ray Vance

Curio by John Nieves

The Rub by Ariana-Sophia Kartsonis

Visiting Indira Gandhi's Palmist by Kirun Kapur

Freaked by Liz Robbins

Looming by Jennifer Franklin

Flammable Matter by Jacob Victorine

Prayer Book of the Anxious by Josephine Yu

flicker by Lisa Bickmore

FICTION

How Things Break by Kerala Goodkin

Nine Ten Again by Phil Condon

Memory Sickness by Phong Nguyen

Troglodyte by Tracy DeBrincat

The Loss of All Lost Things by Amina Gautier